B U N G O
STRAY DOGS
OSAMU DAZAI'S ENTRANCE EXAM

SKILL:
RASHOMON

SKILL:
NO LONGER HUMAN

RYUUNOSUKE
AKUTAGAWA

OSAMU
DAZAI

SKILL:
THE MATCHLESS POET

SKILL:
SUPER DEDUCTION

DOPPO
KUNIKIDA

RANPO
EDOGAWA

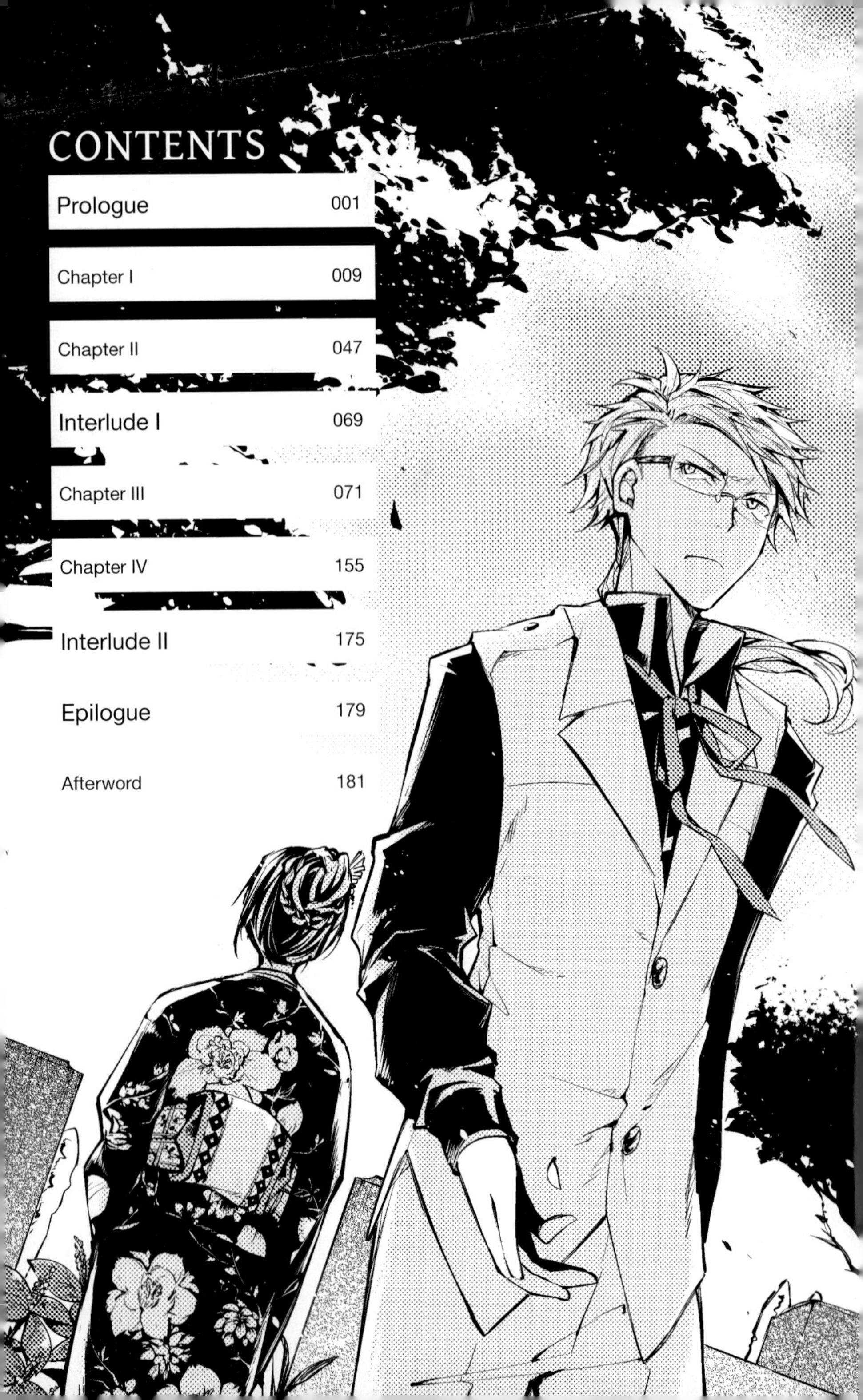

CONTENTS

BUNGO
STRAY DOGS
OSAMU DAZAI'S ENTRANCE EXAM

VOLUME
1

KAFKA ASAGIRI

ILLUSTRATION BY
SANGO HARUKAWA

YEN
ON

NEW YORK

BUNGO STRAY DOGS

VOLUME 1

KAFKA ASAGIRI

Translation by Matt Rutsohn
Cover art by Sango Harukawa

BUNGO STRAY DOGS Vol. 1 DAZAI OSAMU NO NYUSHA SHIKEN
©Kafka Asagiri, Sango Harukawa 2014
First published in JAPAN in 2014 by KADOKAWA CORPORATION, Tokyo.
English translation rights arranged with KADOKAWA CORPORATION, Tokyo through TUTTLE-MORI AGENCY, INC., Tokyo.

English translation © 2019 by Yen Press, LLC

Yen On
1290 Avenue of the Americas
New York, NY 10104

Visit us at yenpress.com • facebook.com/yenpress • twitter.com/yenpress
yenpress.tumblr.com • instagram.com/yenpress

First Yen On Edition: June 2019

Yen On is an imprint of Yen Press, LLC.
The Yen On name and logo are trademarks of Yen Press, LLC.

Library of Congress Cataloging-in-Publication Data
Names: Asagiri, Kafka, author. | Harukawa, Sango, illustrator. | Rutsohn, Matt, translator.
Title: Osamu Dazai's entrance exam / Kafka Asagiri ; illustration by Sango Harukawa ; translation by Matt Rutsohn.
Other titles: Dazai Osamu no nyusha shiken. English
Description: First Yen On edition. | New York, NY : Yen On, 2019. | Series: Bungo stray dogs ; Volume 1
Identifiers: LCCN 2019005328 | ISBN 9781975303228 (pbk.)
Classification: LCC PL867.5.S234 D3913 2019 | DDC 895.63/6—dc23
LC record available at https://lccn.loc.gov/2019005328

ISBNs: 978-1-9753-0322-8 (paperback)
      978-1-9753-0323-5 (ebook)

10 9 8 7 6 5 4 3

LSC-C

Printed in the United States of America

But, look, you can't eat ideals!

—Doppo Kunikida, *Meat and Potatoes*

PROLOGUE

What are *ideals*?

There are innumerable answers to that question. One could say it's merely a term, or an idea, or perhaps even the source of all meaning. But if you ask me, the answer is obvious. It's the word written on the cover of my notebook.

My notebook has all the answers. It is my creed, my master, and a prophet that guides me. At times, it can be either a weapon or a solution.

Ideals.

Everything I am is written in this notebook, which I always carry with me. My entire future lies within it, from what I'm eating for dinner to where I'm moving five years from now, from my list of tomorrow's tasks for work to the cheapest radish prices in the district. My plans, projects, objectives, policies—they're all there, waiting for me to bring them to fruition.

I would even argue that this notebook is like my personal prophecy. My ideals are always inside—all I need to do is follow them. My future is under my control as long as I stick to the plans within this notebook. Control of my future—what promising words.

However—

No matter how brilliant an ideal may be, if the path to

realization is too far, then the light at the end is nothing more than an illusion, and those ideals—meaningless. Thus, the quickest path to fulfillment is inscribed on the first page of my notebook:

"Do what must be done."

My name is Doppo Kunikida, an idealist who lives in reality, a realist who pursues ideals.

And this is a record of the struggles between a man who yearns for the realization of ideals and a new hire destined to interfere with them.

⬡ ⬡ ⬡

7th

Around three days have passed since I wrote a new page in my notebook.

What happened during that time is as follows:

O Takekoshi came to my house. We took a stroll under the moonlight together.

O Hacker Rokuzo Taguchi contacted me back regarding the foreign ship.

O I ate a pear. It wasn't sweet.

I mustn't let petty things bother me.

Ah, I wish for nothing more than to do what is right.

*   *   *

"Stop right there!"

I chase the offender through the city of Yokohama. Mirthful vendors hawking at their stands, crowds of people talking in the streets, customers begging for discounts, and the sound of rickshaws riding east and west over the pavement: The busy shopping arcade is as boisterous as ever. If someone was to start a fight on the right side of the street, the people on the left side wouldn't even notice, I'm sure.

I push through the clamor in pursuit of a criminal, a real *lowlife*. He made a scene at the jewelers' before taking off with some merchandise. Mere baubles, but his third robbery earned him a request for his arrest.

I pursue the criminal after catching him on his fourth offense, but he has a good pair of legs on him, not once slowing down. We pass the market. I continue to cut through the rowdy streets, hunting down my prey until he disappears into a narrow back road.

"You better keep up, newcomer!" I yell to my colleague running behind me.

"Wait, Kunikida! My shoe came untied!"

"Who cares?! Just run!"

Slowly lagging behind is a colleague who just the other day joined our office.

His name: **Osamu Dazai**.

A rather proper-sounding name.

"Phew. Kunikida, I'm exhausted. Could you slow down a little? This isn't good for my health, you know."

"Just pick up the pace, you lazy oaf! My own health is suffering thanks to you!"

"Congratulations!"

"Oh, shut up!"

Osamu Dazai, a man of unknown origin and capabilities, a man most deficient in motivation, lives to throw off my schedule.

He's far too carefree and takes everything at his own pace. To make matters worse, his hobby—

"By the way, Kunikida. Our man is getting away, y'know."

My train of thought interrupted, I look ahead to see the runaway mow down a street vendor's vegetables before taking a left to escape. I instinctively click my tongue. Then I dive into my memories to recall a map of the area. He's heading toward a narrow residential district with hedges lining each side of the street. There are countless houses to escape to or hide in around that area.

"You see that, Dazai?! Thanks to your dawdling, he's now going to be even harder to catch!"

"Don't worry about it. It's all according to plan. More importantly, guess what I just saw."

"I don't care!"

"It's this incredibly rare book called *The Complete Suicide*. I've been searching all over for it, and I just noticed it on display in the used bookstore back there— Ah! I have to go back and buy it before someone else does."

Nobody asked.

"I could always just shoot you in the head if you want to die that badly!" I yell, to which he replies:

"Wait. Seriously? Wow, thanks."

He smiles bashfully, even though there's nothing to blush about.

For a man who doesn't put much effort into his job, he sure puts a lot of work into fantasizing about suicide. It's a world unfamiliar to me. However, there isn't a waking moment when he isn't searching for the cheapest, quickest way to off himself. He's obsessed with suicide.

A suicide aficionado?

How vile.

But no matter how twisted my partner's interests are, no matter how much he tries to sabotage the mission, I will not allow the criminal to escape, for *failure* is not written in my schedule.

I chase the lowlife into a dark path wide enough for only one person at a time. Both sides are lined with hedges, and I can see a well and the backyard of an old house. A washing machine lies knocked over under the roof's eaves. I open a map of the area on my mobile device, and a white dot representing our location is displayed along with the buildings and backstreets.

Narrow paths branch out in every direction through the residential district. If the thief keeps heading straight, he'll most likely make his way to the old factory district, filled with premodern warehouses. We would have an easier time finding a needle in a haystack than finding him there.

The criminal slowly fades into the distance.

Looks like he really is heading toward the old factory district.

"Damn it!"

The foul curse slips off my tongue. I won't be able to catch up when I'm this far behind. And he would no doubt repeat the crime if he is allowed to get away. It would put our client's business at risk while even further damaging our detective agency's image.

What should I do? What *can* I do?

"Well then, I think it's about time we end this so I can go buy that book. We just need to slow him down, right?"

Dazai breaks into a smile.

Then he takes in a deep breath before yelling in a booming voice:

"Fire!!"

The townspeople immediately lunge into the streets in a panic, blocking the criminal's path of escape. People nearby come rushing out in utter confusion: a woman holding a pot lid, a young man with sleepy eyes, an elderly fellow carrying his shogi board. People crowd the streets one after another, making it impossible to get by.

The criminal is at his wits' end. The path is overrun with people, meaning going back is no longer an option, either. Verbal threats wouldn't work against a crowd desperately searching for the fire, and an open door now further blocks the offender's path of return.

"How's that?"

"You idiot! Yes, you stopped him, but it doesn't matter if we can't get to him!"

"Sure we can! I mean, that's why we have the skilled detective Doppo Kunikida with us, right? I set the stage, so now it's your turn to show us what you've got."

I'm going to sew those lips of yours shut before long!

I open my notebook and quickly jot something down. After ripping out the page with the words WIRE GUN inscribed, I infuse it with my will.

"The Matchless Poet!"

My special skill.

I don't know how I do it, and I can't logically explain how it works. All I can say is *that's just how it is.* There is no rational explanation for why it has to be a page out of my notebook or how it can transform in spite of the laws of physics.

The sheet of paper transforms into a wire gun *exactly as written.* I leap onto a nearby fence before pointing the muzzle at the thief. That's when I notice him reaching for a gun in his pocket to threaten the citizens blocking his way.

You know something is wrong with the world when even a lowlife crook in the outskirts of town has a gun.

At any rate, I can't let him use it in such a densely populated area!

I aim, then pull the trigger. A harpoon-shaped hook shoots out toward the target with a steel wire trailing behind. Before the thief can even lift his arm completely, the hook knocks the gun out of his hand, then pierces his sleeve, tethering him to the wall behind.

"Jackpot." Dazai offers a pathetic attempt at a whistle.

I reel in the steel wire while kicking off one fence and landing on another, repeating the movement to make my way forward. After jumping over the heads of the townspeople, I land right in front of the fugitive.

As I lift my head, he takes out a dagger he was hiding in his pocket. He swings the weapon not even three feet away, but the blade of an amateur has no chance of hitting me. I casually tilt my head to the side, then gently grab his elbow and wrist. With the help of his momentum, I twist his wrist while pushing the elbow in the opposite direction to send him flying into the air. He makes an arc in the sky before slamming upside down into the wall. His face contorts in surprise as if he doesn't know what just happened. Then he falls to the ground and passes out.

It's a throwing technique that uses the opponent's momentum against them.

The area residents look back and forth between the thief and me in mute amazement. Soon after, Dazai finally catches up before addressing the crowd.

"Our sincere apologies for all the fuss, ladies and gentlemen. However, there is no longer any need to worry. Oh, and the fire was a false alarm."

One resident speaks up. "J-just who are you people?"

I whip out my detective license and hold it up in the air so everyone can see.

"There is no need for concern. We're with the Armed Detective Agency."

CHAPTER I

8th

It rained this morning.

A quiet shower, but frigid like the depths of winter.

I yearn to live for my ideals.

I strive for my ideals. I move forward without fear, without fatigue, without hesitation.

Neither dreams nor honor will be pursued—for how euphoric it can be to solely devote oneself to quotidian tasks.

The Armed Detective Agency's office sits at the top of a slope near Yokohama's port. It's a reddish-brown brick building with years of wear and tear, and its rain gutters and lampposts are sheathed in rust from the rough sea breeze. But despite its appearance, it's so sturdily built that even machine-gun artillery fire from the outside wouldn't cause any damage to the interior. That may sound oddly specific, but it's happened to us.

In any event, our detective agency is situated on the fourth floor. The other floors are occupied by proper tenants. There's a café on the first floor and a law firm on the second. The third is vacant, and the fifth is used for miscellaneous storage. The café takes good care of me right before payday comes, and I'm at the law firm asking for help every time there's some legal trouble at work.

I take the building's elevator to the fourth floor, get off, and stand before the office. On the door is a plate with the words ARMED DETECTIVE AGENCY written in simple, fine brushstrokes. I check my watch. I still have forty seconds before work starts at eight o'clock.

Looks like I got here a little early.

Punctuality is my philosophy. Flipping through my notebook as I wait, I double-check today's schedule. I already checked once during breakfast, once after leaving the dormitory, and once while waiting for the light to change, but I've never heard of anyone dying from excessive confirmation of their schedule. I read my notebook, ruminating on my work plans, then glance at my watch one more time as I adjust my shirt collar.

…*Perfect.*

"Good morning."

I open the door.

"Oh, Kunikida! Good morning! Take a look at this! It's incredible!"

I'm suddenly greeted by a grinning Dazai on the threshold.

"At last, I've made it! Ah, and what a sweet world it is! This is Yomotsu Hirasaka, the gateway to the afterlife! Look, it's just as I imagined! The blue smoke covering the surface, the moonlight peeking in through the window, the pink elephant dancing in the westerly skies…!"

He dances in front of the office door with wild gesticulations.

What a pain in the ass.

"Heh-heh-heh-heh! I just knew that *Complete Suicide* book would be a masterpiece! And to think, all it took to achieve such a simple yet pleasurable suicide was to ingest a mushroom growing along the mountain path! How wonderful! Ah-ha-ha!"

Dazai's eyes are slightly twitching and unfocused.

"K-Kunikida, please do something!" a staff member begs, teary-eyed.

I guess it's safe to assume that Dazai's been like this all morning. I glance at his desk and see the blasphemous book he bought the other day, *The Complete Suicide*, opened to a page titled "Death by Poisoning: Mushrooms." Next to the book lies a plate with a half-eaten mushroom on it. However, upon further inspection, it appears to be a slightly different color from the one in the book.

"Come, Kunikida! Join me in the underworld! See, here the alcohol flows freely, and you can help yourself to as much food as you'd like! You can sniff beautiful women until you're blue in the face!"

"Please help, Kunikida; we've tried everything we could..."

Quite simply, the mushroom he ingested wasn't the fatal kind but rather the *hallucinogenic* type.

However, that doesn't matter to me.

I always do things in the same order each and every morning. If I didn't follow my morning schedule as planned, would I still be able to finish my day's work on time? The answer is no. I head to my desk, ignoring my crying coworker and that prancing imbecile. I set down my bag just as I always do. I boot up my computer and, as per usual, open the window.

"Whoa! There's a giant sea anemone outside the window, Kunikida! A banana... It's eating a banana! And it's even removing the white stringy bits!"

I pour coffee into my mug just as I always do. Then I dispose of any documents from yesterday's work that are no longer needed.

"Oh, I've got it. I need to take off my clothes. I need to get naked to get higher ratings! It's simple, really! Let us undress! After that, we can all put on full-body tights, go to the bank, and dance the hopak!"

I check the telegraph rack just like always, then take a sip of my coffee.

"I can hear voices... Ohhh...! They're in— They're in my head! ...The tiny man is whispering to me to go to Kyoto! That's where they have the best miso tofu—"

I land a roundhouse kick to the back of Dazai's head, knocking him against the wall and rendering him unconscious.

⬡ ⬡ ⬡

It was only four days ago when this failure of a human being became my colleague.

"A new employee?"

That day, I had been filing some paperwork when the president called me into his office.

He told me they had hired a new investigator, so he wanted me to look after him.

It was unexpected. Admittedly, the Armed Detective Agency profits from violence and deals with life-threatening work, but I've never heard anything about being short on staff. I'm even able to hold a second job working as an algebra instructor at Shin-Tsuruya Institute twice a week.

Granted, there has been an increase in cases that require armed personnel, such as the "Azure Banner Terrorist," the "Serial Disappearances of Yokohama Visitors," and our feud with the underground organization known as the Port Mafia. Honestly, we've been getting so many dangerous job offers of late that even our top detective, Ranpo, would have a hard time covering them all on his own. Perhaps the president hired a new employee in anticipation of that.

"Let me introduce you. Come in."

The president faces the door after a few moments of contemplation and calls out to someone.

"Good afternoon."

A man smiles from ear to ear as he enters the room.

He's wearing a sand-colored coat and an open-collared shirt. He's tall and thin with disheveled black hair, and while his unkempt appearance leaves much to be desired, he has somewhat handsome features. I am slightly curious about the white bandages wrapped around his neck and wrists, though.

"I'm Osamu Dazai, twenty years old. Nice to meet you."

Twenty, huh? He's the same age as me.

"I'm Kunikida. If there's anything you don't understand, I'm here to help."

"Oh, so you're a detective at the legendary Armed Detective Agency! It's an honor to meet you!"

He forcefully grabs my hand and shakes it in an exaggerated manner.

In that moment, I suddenly sense a cold, piercing light in his eyes, as if he were calmly evaluating his senior—no, as if he were staring into my very soul through the eyes of a heavenly, enlightened sage. However, it is only for a fleeting moment before his vacant expression returns. Was I seeing things? Could my mind have been playing tricks on me? I pull myself together.

"So, Dazai, what brings you to our detective agency? This kind of place won't take in just anyone who asks."

"Yes, about that. I was at this pub—bored, unemployed—drunkenly complaining to myself when I happened to hit it off with some old guy sitting next to me. He said he'd give me a job if I beat him in a drinking contest. And, well, I jokingly went along with it but ended up winning."

Who is this "old guy"?

"It was Chief Taneda of the Special Division for Unusual Powers. He came by yesterday and gave me the news," the president says with a straight face.

I find myself speechless when I hear him mention Chief Taneda's name so casually. Chief Taneda is the top brass in the Home Affairs Ministry's Special Division for Unusual Powers, a secret military agency unknown to the general public. His job is to control and regulate information on skill users. I've even heard he provided support to our president in establishing the Armed Detective Agency. That's why not even the president himself can refuse such a referral.

"I really hope we can get along, Kunikida."

Our new hire gives me a toothy smile, perhaps oblivious of my internal apprehension.

○ ○ ○

However, being personally recommended by a prominent figure doesn't make you any less of a nuisance when you're tripping on mushrooms this early in the morning.

Today marks three days since I was paired with Dazai.

I'm mentally exhausted, almost no work is getting done, and we're receiving more complaints by the day. If I take my eyes off him for even a second, he'll either leap into a river and claim he was trying to drown himself; get blackout drunk at a pub after what he calls a "pick-me-up"; or chat up some pretty lady, saying he had a divine revelation. He's a twenty-year-old self-centered man-child who throws a wrench in my schedule every chance he gets.

Having said that, work is work, and coworkers are coworkers. Admitting defeat after only three days would damage not only the president's trust in me but my dignity as a detective as well.

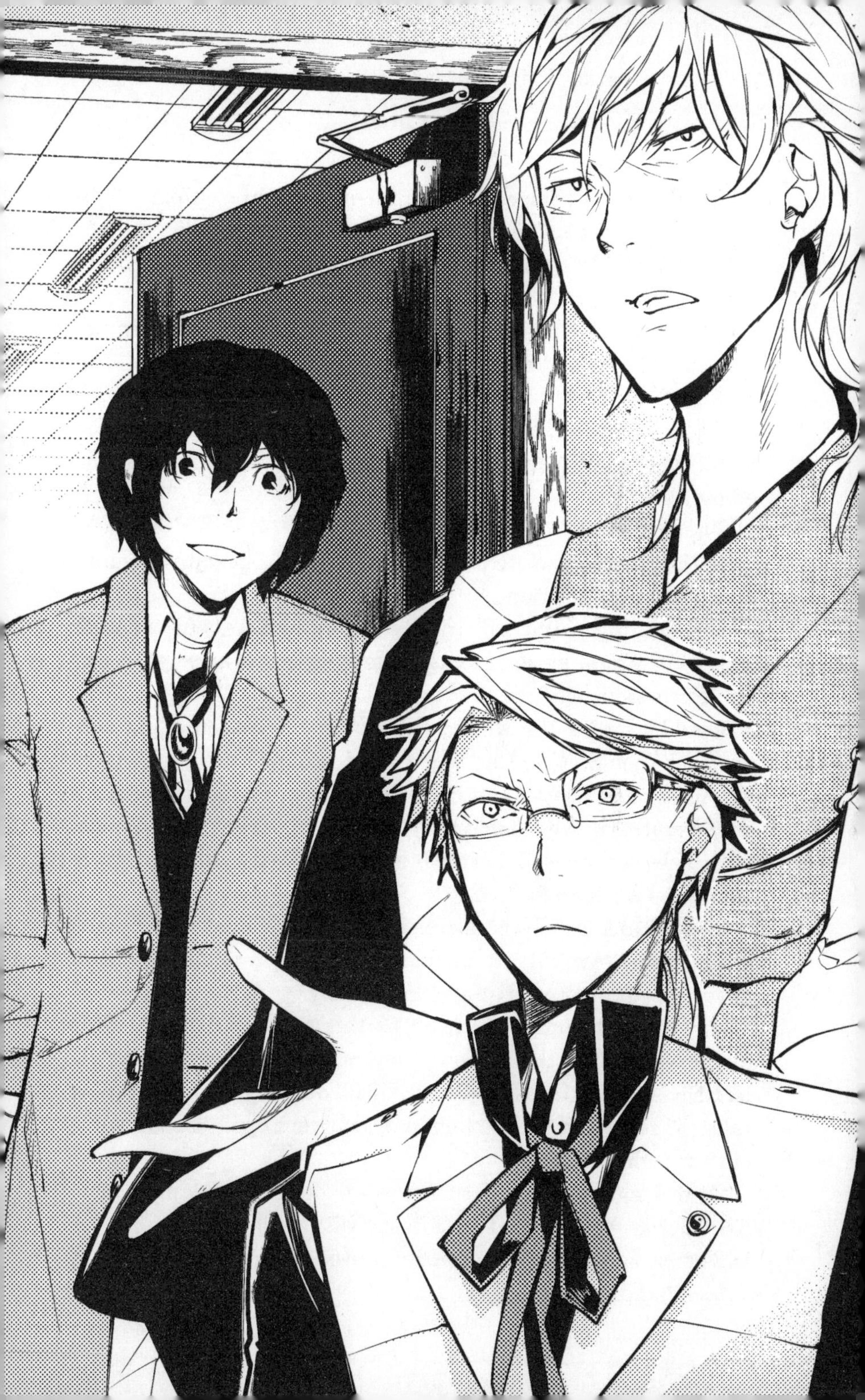

"How's the newcomer?" the president asks while we play Go in a small tatami room near the office.

"A disaster. Imagine the devil, a poltergeist, and the god of poverty all combined into one entity."

I place a black Go piece on the cypress board with the distinctive *click* of rock sliding over wood.

"But it's nothing I can't handle."

The president and I always play Go at the same place after work. He sits up straight, facing me from across the board in the empty room.

"I appreciate it."

He then places a white Go piece on the board, pushing me into an unfavorable position.

"It's nothing. After all, this is what Chief Taneda wanted. But...why would he send a man like that to our agency?" I ask while contemplating my next move.

Should I go for the white territory in the bottom right corner? ...I shouldn't. I'm having a hard enough time making an approach move as it is. But if I try to hold out on the left side, it's only a matter of time before he takes the center and the game is over. There's nothing I can do. It looks like it's going to be a while before I'm a match for him.

"Chief Taneda may be a free-spirited individual, but he has a discerning eye when it comes to remarkable talent. He must have sensed something unique in that boy."

I have heard rumors about his extraordinary judgment. After all, he wouldn't be the leader of the Home Affairs Ministry's Special Division for Unusual Powers if he didn't. But "remarkable talent"? You could shine a light in Dazai's left ear and see it come out the right.

"And I agree with Chief Taneda's decision. Osamu Dazai passed the written and field tests with perfect scores. He is extremely capable—dangerously so, even."

"...What do you mean?"

"We looked into his past but found nothing. It's completely blank. I asked a close friend in the military's intelligence department to check, but he couldn't find a single thing. Rather eerie, I must say. It's as if someone very carefully wiped his background clean."

It is rather odd that even the military's intelligence department couldn't find anything.

"Maybe all he did was loaf around the house for the past twenty years?"

"Perhaps. Because otherwise…"

He frowns even deeper than usual before continuing.

"Have you heard about his skill?"

"Not yet."

I heard he was a skill user, but I didn't get the chance to ask about it.

"He can nullify any skill simply through physical contact."

I thought I was hearing things. Nullify skills on contact? At a glance, it may seem like nothing special, but it's extremely rare. If properly utilized, it could be used to defeat an entire organization of skill users. My skill, *The Matchless Poet*, allows me to materialize objects just by writing them in my notebook, ripping out the page, and willing them into existence. However, I cannot produce items larger than the notebook itself. While it's versatile and highly valuable, it doesn't quite exceed the realm of convenience. That's because if I really needed something, I could simply bring it with me before I went out.

But Dazai's skill is different. In theory, there are countless enemies only he can defeat. Even the strongest skill user in the world is nothing more than an ordinary person before him. It would be no surprise if organizations from all over the world gathered to recruit him. I'm slowly starting to get what the president is trying to say.

"So…let me get this straight. At some pub, a tremendously important man like Chief Taneda just happens to sit next to a genius skill user, and they just happen to hit it off. Then this oddball happens to be sharp and gets a perfect score on his tests, but he also just happens to currently not have a job. Then, just like that, he successfully joins the prohibitively selective Armed Detective Agency without any trouble at all... Are you implying this is all a little *too* convenient?"

"Perhaps I am overthinking things, but the Armed Detective Agency has numerous connections with government agencies and military personnel. We also handle a large amount of classified information due to the nature of our work."

It would make sense for a member of a criminal organization to infiltrate a detective agency due to their close ties to the police. There are plenty of advantages in joining a detective agency, given how easy some are to get into. But Dazai, a spy? And one good enough to outwit someone as distinguished as Chief Taneda? *That* Dazai?

"Kunikida, I want you to carry out his entrance exam."

I nod. The agency's "entrance exam" is a task assigned to detectives to give to prospective employees. It's the real test, so to speak, and you will not be recognized as an actual employee if you don't pass.

"I would like you to bring Dazai with you while you work and see if he can be trusted. If you ever feel he could be an emissary, intelligence operative, or spy of some sort, then you are to fire him without hesitation. However, if you sense any signs of wickedness in his heart..."

The president takes a black automatic pistol out from a bag behind him, then presents it to me.

"..."

I accept the gun without a word. It's heavy.

"Shoot him."

"Yes, sir."

If Dazai is part of some sinister scheme, then it would be the agency's duty to stop him before things got out of hand. The Armed Detective Agency's licensed staff are granted police-like authority. We're authorized to carry guns and knives under certain conditions, and we can even pull records from police organizations. But above all, it allows us to commit unethical acts if we wish to do so: meddle with said authorities' investigations, falsify police information, and even wiretap or secretly film key facilities. At worst, one could even commit an act of terrorism and sabotage these major facilities, resulting in the deaths of hundreds—if not thousands of individuals.

The cold iron pistol sits motionless in my hand.

◯　◯　◯

Rippling waves roll over the bay beneath a shower of moonlight as I walk through the crowd by the Port of Yokohama. The sound of the ocean struggles to be heard over the hustle and bustle of the evening, while the moon competes with the city lights. Dazai slowly bobs down the street behind me.

We're finally able to start work after he wasted half a day with the whole mushroom fiasco.

"Hey, show me that skill of yours again. *The Matchless Poet*, was it?"

"No. One doesn't so casually reveal his skill. Besides, I have to tear a page out of my notebook every time I use it. The artisan who makes these notebooks produces only a hundred of them a year, and they're not cheap. Do you really think I'm going to waste a page just to entertain you?"

I check my watch before looking back at him.

"Anyway, Dazai, you need to walk a little faster. We're going to be late."

"What do you mean, late? I thought we didn't set a specific time to meet up with the informant?"

"No, I told them over the phone that we'd be there around seven PM."

"Well, it's exactly seven now, and they're only about five minutes from here, so we won't be late."

"That means we're already late, you idiot! According to my watch, 'around seven PM' refers to the twenty seconds between 18:59:50 and 19:00:10!"

"You're the only one with a watch like that, Kunikida...," Dazai mumbles as he walks.

Incidentally, my watch uses specialized equipment to set itself to standard time every morning when I wake up, so the margin of error is always under one second.

"We would've been done with most of our work today if a certain someone hadn't eaten a magic mushroom. Don't you dare eat one of those again. And if you do, make sure it's the fatal kind."

"Ah, what a pleasurable experience that was."

"You're fine now, right? Still seeing pink elephants in the sky?"

"Elephants? Don't be silly—elephants can't fly. Those were purple elephant *beetles* I was seeing."

There's no hope for this guy. The more I talk to him, the more foolish I feel for ever having doubts about him. A spy? Wickedness in his heart? The worst he could do is jump in front of a train and screw up the rail schedule. At any rate, if Dazai does end up being nothing more than an incompetent fool, then the solution is simple. I just have to get rid of him, which I would be more than happy to do. But—

"Dazai, you remember our mission, right?"

"Exterminating the purple elephant beetles."

"...You know, I kind of get the feeling you're doing this on purpose."

"Ah-ha-ha. I kid. We're going to investigate a haunted mansion, right?"

His smiling face and casual demeanor cause me to scowl.

Yesterday, I received an e-mail with a request from a client. The message said the following:

Dear Sir,

I hope everyone at the Armed Detective Agency is doing well. I am contacting you in hopes of asking you a favor. I understand that you are very busy. However, I was left with no other choice.

    To tell the truth, I would like you to investigate a certain building. It should be completely uninhabited, yet night after night, I hear eerie groaning and whispering coming from within, and I see a faint light flickering through the window. The other neighboring residents and I are so terribly frightened, we can hardly sleep.

    I understand that this is not a small request, but I would be forever in your debt if you could check to see whether this is some sort of prank. Moreover, if this does happen to be a prank, then I would appreciate it if you could explain how and why it is occurring.

    While it is not much, I sent you a retainer fee for your services, so please have a look at your earliest convenience. Furthermore, I ask that this request remain a secret between us. Thank you for your understanding.

I wish everyone good health and the best of luck.

Yours sincerely.

It's a rather long-winded request, but its sender is essentially asking us to check out a building in their neighborhood to see what all the strange noises are. Almost immediately after this e-mail arrived, the agency received a letter in the mail containing the retainer fee. I verified the amount to find that it was twice the market rate even after subtracting the planned expenses, which gave us no reason to refuse. We will conduct our business as per usual.

There is one thing I'm worried about, though: *The client didn't leave a name.* It is not clear who they are, where they live, or even how to get in touch with them. Perhaps that was intentional, but we won't be able to report our findings if we cannot contact them. Thus, we have no choice but to search for the client first.

"What if the client's some kind of vengeful spirit? Perhaps they've tricked us into coming to this haunted mansion to eat us, and—"

"You fool. What kind of ghost story involves vengeful spirits writing e-mails?"

And I wouldn't be afraid if it ended up being a ghost anyway.

As we continue our idle banter, we end up heading to the warehouses at the port. The moonlight reflects off the brick warehouses, dimly illuminating the cluster of buildings under the blanket of night. We step foot into an old warehouse that's a size smaller than the rest. The ceiling is high, and the plaster on the walls is peeling due to the ocean breeze. My nose is tickled by the smell of iron machine parts and oil along with the old scent of dust and the passage of time. I ring the office doorbell. There's a creaking sound as if iron is sliding against iron, and the electronic lock clicks open.

"C'mon in."

Sure enough, a high-pitched voice welcomes us inside. We pass through a few heavy birch doors that have been unlocked remotely before arriving at our destination.

The room is just shy of 380 square feet. Machinery and electronics run across the floor and up the walls, the blinking diodes illuminating the dusky room. In the center stands a collection of computers with fans whirring like growling wolves. There are four LCD panels on the desk, each emitting a pale-blue light.

"Heya, Four-Eyes. Still religiously following that little notebook of yours?"

"Is that really the tone you want to take with me, informant? If we hand over the evidence we have on you, like we should, you'd be looking at ten years in prison. And that would break your late father's heart."

"Don't you dare bring my dad into this."

The informant, a fourteen-year-old boy, stacks his legs on the desk before leaning back in his chair. Cropped hair, big eyes, always wears the same white sweater no matter the season. He may be small, but his vision is sharp enough to cut glass.

"Anyway, it's not like you to be late. What, were you on a 'date' or somethin'?"

He makes a circle with one hand and shoves a finger in it with the other.

"Sorry to disappoint, but I only plan on going on dates with the woman I marry. And according to the 'Future Plans' page in my notebook," I reply as I turn to the appropriate page, "it's going to be another six years before I get married."

"Hold up. You already got a girl you're gonna marry?"

"Not for another four years."

"Uh-huh…"

The boy's eyes fly open, and his jaw drops when he realizes I'm serious.

"Take a good look, lad. I live according to my ideals and schedule. That's what it means to be an adult."

"Yeah… I've got a pretty good idea what kinda person you are, but that was…uh, *something*."

Dazai passes through the door behind me.

"Hmm? Who's the new guy?"

"Hey there. I'd love to introduce myself, but I'd rather not listen to Kunikida's sass afterward."

"You should introduce yourself first before asking, lad. Oh, and, Dazai, don't try to guess what I'm going to do unless I give you express permission."

"Geez, Four-Eyes. You sure love bossing people around… Whatever. Name's Rokuzo Taguchi, age fourteen. I'm a professional hacker."

"He's the idiot who tried to hack into our system and was caught, so I had to teach him some manners." I graciously add a few comments for clarity.

"C'mon, that was forever ago. Just gimme the logs already."

Rokuzo hacked into the Armed Detective Agency's information archive three months ago and threw the organization into chaos. Naturally, the agency is prepared for cyberattacks, and we traced the hacker back here. I roughed up Rokuzo a bit, and now he's working as our information broker on the condition that we don't hand the logs over to the police as incriminating evidence. It's a symbiotic relationship.

"So did you figure out who sent us that e-mail I asked you to look into?"

"Wow. Impatient much? I literally just saw it. I'm gonna need more time."

I had asked him to locate the mysterious sender. Tracing an e-mail surely isn't a difficult task for someone of Rokuzo's caliber.

"Besides, I'm already busy tracing the missing persons you asked me to find. Isn't that more important?"

"It is." I nod in agreement.

He's referring to the Serial Disappearances of Yokohama Visitors case.

There has been a series of missing-persons incidents, with no obvious connections among the victims. Eleven people have gone missing by now, and already a month has passed since a formal criminal investigation was launched. The victims have only two things in common, albeit minor: They don't live in Yokohama, and they *walked off into thin air.* It's a difficult case with no clues that would help us know where to even begin searching. What I asked Rokuzo to do was to track down evidence of the victims' activity before they went missing, such as footage of them getting on a train or taking a taxi. However, the results have been less than ideal.

"Wait. Who went missing? Nobody's told me anything about this." Dazai chimes in, expressing interest.

"I'll explain everything later."

However, I casually brush him off—with reason, of course. I plan to make solving this case Dazai's entrance exam, and I want to wait for the right time before disclosing said information.

"Ooh, training the newbie, huh? You've really moved up in the ranks, Four-Eyes."

"Yeah, he's a real stubborn boss. You wouldn't believe what I put up with... By the way, Rokuzo, was it? You're a hacker, right? So you got any dirt on Kunikida? Maybe some incriminating photos?"

"Dazai! Not a wise move scheming to blackmail me when I'm right here!"

"Heh. I like your style, new guy. We got the thousand-yen plan, the ten-thousand-yen plan, and the hundred-thousand-yen plan. What's it gonna be?"

"Just what do you have on me?!"

Wait, wait, wait. Relax, Doppo.

"Don't make me laugh. I have nothing to hide. Dazai, ignore this kid. He's bluffing."

"...Hmm." Dazai shoots me a meaningful glance.

"You don't have to believe me. I'll just sell the information to customers who do. I mean, I guess I could always dispose of it if you're willing to cough up the cash, Four-Eyes."

"Keep dreaming! No such information exists! Come on, Dazai! We're leaving!"

I grab Dazai by the collar and quickly drag him out of the room, leaving the information broker's hideout.

...One hundred and eleven thousand yen...?

⬡ ⬡ ⬡

There is not a soul to be seen in the old factory district. Dazai and I stand in the street, waiting for the taxi we called. Trails of light from passing vehicles come and go. A splash of yellow. A silver ribbon. The scattered crimson of brake lights. White headlights cut through the buildings' shadows. The reflections of streetlamps flow across the car windows like water. The strong ocean winds slowly push the clouds away, allowing the moonlight to cast black shadows and white highlights over the port.

"He's a good kid," Dazai says with a grin as he looks up at the night sky.

"I made a mistake by introducing you two. I should have known it wouldn't lead to anything good."

"Hey, can I ask you something?"

"What?"

"Why are you looking after him?"

I glance at Dazai, noticing his solemn expression.

"Why would you ask him for help? The agency surely doesn't need any assistance tracing missing people. Plus, you could have just called him for that."

I don't say a word. It's a difficult question.

"Would it maybe have something to do with this father of his you mentioned?"

I can't help myself from turning to face him.

"Thought so."

Dazai smiles, taking note of my expression.

"...Rokuzo's father was an accomplished police officer before he died," I begin to explain reluctantly. "Some time ago, the agency worked together with the police to track down a certain criminal. He was a big shot—as bad as they come. He destroyed numerous national and corporate buildings. Even though the police were doing everything they could to find him, they just couldn't trace the guy."

"Are you talking about the Azure Banner Terrorist?"

"Yes."

It turned into a heinous case that shook the country, involving both the military and the police.

"After much time, our agency finally succeeded in finding his hideout, which we reported to the city police."

"That's amazing," Dazai replies, impressed.

"Yeah, it was a big deal. However, at the time, the case was being handled by the military, the security police, and the city police as a joint effort, which caused mass confusion among the multiple chains of command. To make matters worse, the criminal got wind of what we were doing, so he barricaded himself in his hideout along with a large number of high-powered explosives."

It's all coming back to me. Conflicting orders coming from all directions—some telling us to arrest the target, some telling us to stand by...

"Because of the chaotic orders, only five detectives were able to promptly make it to the scene. They were told to rush in and neutralize the enemy at once... But what could five ordinary detectives, neither skill users nor special ops, hope to accomplish against the bloodthirsty Azure King?"

Not only that, but those on the ground have no way of grasping the situation in its entirety. If the higher-ups give orders to rush in, then that's it.

"After being driven into a corner, the Azure King set off a bomb, killing himself...along with the five detectives."

"...And one of those police officers happened to be Rokuzo's father, huh?"

"Rokuzo lost his mother at a young age. It was just him and his father after that, and he seemed to really look up to the man." I clench my fist. "I was the one who contacted the police and told them we found the terrorist's hideout."

If only I had contacted someone higher up on the chain of

command... If only the detective agency had stormed the hideout with them...

"I as good as killed him."

"No, you didn't. It was the higher-ups at the police station who gave the orders, and besides, the criminal's the one who blew himself up."

"That may be true, but I doubt the lad sees it that way. He wouldn't have tried getting revenge by hacking into the detective agency's database otherwise."

I suspect Rokuzo resents us. I've never asked him face-to-face, but...

"Rokuzo's father is gone, and nothing is going to change that. That's why somebody needs to look out for him—keep him in line when he acts out. And I just happen to be in a position to do it. It's a matter of convenience."

"You're a real romanticist, you know that?" Dazai's snickering comes out sounding like a sigh. I've never considered myself to be a romanticist, nor do I really know what it means to be sentimental. However, my acquaintances do often describe me as such, though I can't understand why. After all, this world is far from ideal.

A taxi stops in front of us while I ponder. The driver waves.

⬡ ⬡ ⬡

No two taxi drivers are the same. Some are upstanding people; some are sincere. Some know the side streets and shortcuts like the back of their hand, and some are expert motorists. You've also got your cheerful young taxi drivers, along with the more frugal ones who keep their eye on the meter at all times. There is no one answer to which is best, and everyone is rightfully entitled to their opinion. However, there is only one thing I hope for when I get inside a taxi.

"Well, long time no see, Detective Kunikida. We're having such nice weather today, yes? It really is the perfect day for investigating. Your glasses really suit you; then again, they always do. When you've driven cabs for as long as I have, you start to notice who does and doesn't look good in glasses. You can see if they're refined, whether they come from good stock. And your glasses are very becoming! Yep, I guarantee it."

"Please, could you shut up and just drive?"

Besides, how can you determine a person's upbringing just from their glasses? Ridiculous... I am slightly curious, though.

"The best taxi drivers are the ones who don't talk. Has nobody ever told you that before?"

"Never. In fact, the passengers never really tell me anything at all when I'm driving, since I'm talking the whole time."

I know what they call a taxi driver like this: a chatterbox.

Dazai and I are taking the cab to our next destination for investigation. I look out the window to discover the absence of lights. Shadows from the sparsely distributed trees brush away the dim moonlight as they fade into the distance. Needless to say, it wasn't a stroke of misfortune that we happened to get into this taxi. We specifically asked for this driver. Why?

To get information.

"Dazai, you know the missing-persons case I mentioned earlier?"

"You mean the one Rokuzo's looking into?"

"Precisely. Eleven people are missing so far. And this driver saw two of them right before they disappeared."

I point at the small-framed individual driving the vehicle.

"All I did was drive them from the port to their hotel, though. One was a woman on vacation, while the other was a man in Yokohama on business."

"Are you sure these are the two people you saw?"

I pull out a few pictures from my pocket. They're all photos of the victims, taken by the hotel's security camera. There are three types: when they're entering the building, when they're filling out the paperwork at the counter, and from the next day when they're leaving the hotel.

"Yes, that's them all right. They were wearing those same clothes. I drove them to this hotel, too."

"Great. So, Kunikida, can you finally fill me in on the case's details?"

"...Very well."

I then begin to summarize the case. About a month ago, a forty-two-year-old man was visiting Yokohama on business when he suddenly vanished. After tracing his footsteps, it became clear that he left the port, checked into the hotel, and went to town the next day. However, he never showed up to his work meeting, nor did he ever return home. His belongings were still in the hotel room, and he simply left of his own accord, disappearing without a trace.

A single traveler, a participant in a trade show—the other missing people vanished more or less the same way. From age to place of residence and workplace, none of the eleven victims has anything in common, barring that they all visited Yokohama alone. The city police are asking around town, trying to trace the victims' footsteps after they left the hotel, but they've yet to find any witnesses. It's as if these people disappeared like a puff of smoke.

The police are leaning toward the possibility of a kidnapping. However, there isn't a single place in this massive city where someone could be abducted without any witnesses. What would be their objective anyway? None of the families has been threatened to pay a ransom or anything of the sort.

"The objective's pretty clear if you ask me."

Dazai, who had been quiet this entire time, suddenly speaks up with a merry note in his voice.

"Trade."

"What?"

"I'm saying, somebody's kidnapping these people and selling them. From what I've heard, it sounds like the missing people have all been healthy adults, right? Hearts, kidneys, corneas, lungs, livers, pancreases, bone marrow—I mean, they'd all be sold in foreign markets, so they're not particularly valuable in terms of yen, but having eleven bodies is like stepping into a gold mine. If the criminal is acting alone, then I bet they're sitting on a fortune."

"I've heard about black markets like this before, but how do you know so much about them?"

I'm fairly sure the general public knows only what they see in movies or hear in stories.

"Oh, y'know, I just heard people talking about it at this dingy pub outside of town once."

How convenient. A sketchy excuse at best. Then again, the very atoms that make up his body are suspect.

"...So you're telling me the victims went to the buyer themselves? In the middle of their trip, they went out of their way to beg someone to buy their organs?"

"Yeah, you're right. It doesn't add up. I guess that means they just wanted to disappear for some reason? Maybe they met with a mediator who specializes in taking people and giving them new names and identities."

"But then there should be witnesses or security footage proving they left town to meet with the mediator."

"What if they went to a master of disguise to alter their appearance?"

"Now that you mention it, I've heard of someone like that before! In show business, they have this technique that can change men into women. Like, first, they fill their cheeks with some sort of cotton to change the shape of their face, and then—"

"Nobody asked you." I promptly cut off the driver before he launches into another one of his never-ending stories.

"Ah, I've got it! Look at this picture! They're both wearing glasses, right? I found something they have in common! It's the case of the Serial Disappearances of People with Glasses!"

I take a look. The victims are indeed wearing glasses: one with black frames and one with silver.

"This is your chance, Kunikida!"

"My chance to do what? Regardless, several of the victims weren't wearing glasses, you know. So no, you didn't find something they all have in common."

If my memory serves me correctly, four of the other nine victims were wearing prescription glasses, two were wearing sunglasses, and three were wearing nothing at all.

"Tsk... Guess I'll just have to come up with another way to use you as bait. I bet the criminal targets tourists. All right, Kunikida, slip on your rubber boots, throw on your backpack, put on your red-and-green-striped shirt, and start walking the town in your knickerbockers. Make sure to bring a giant camera with you to take pictures of everyone who walks by and say 'eh' at the end of every sentence."

"Like hell I will!"

"'Like hell I will, eh!'"

"You call that a strategy? That's a terri—"

"'A terrible idea, eh?'"

"Stop guessing what I'm going to say!"

"Hmm? In that case, how about you get naked, put on a top hat, and ride around on a unicycle screaming what kind of girls you like?"

"We're not even talking about the same thing anymore!"

"Hey, I have an idea, too, Detective Kunikida. How about you dress up like a clown and read—?"

"You stay out of this!"

Argh, the both of them! I'm slowly starting to lose my temper here.

"Dazai! When are you going to start taking work seriously?! Get it together!"

"What? But I always take work seriously."

I really hope that's just a bad joke.

"Okay, how about this: Starting real soon, I vow to become a detective you can count on. I will carefully and thoroughly investigate, examine, and reach logical deductions based on evidence. After that, you'll be so impressed that you'll immediately allow me to start investigating on my own, and my amazing detective skills will bring a tear to your eye." Dazai rattles on, trying to persuade me, but his babbling means little to me.

"And how soon is 'real soon'?"

"Right after we get out of this taxi."

Oh?

"Is that so?"

"Indeed it is. A suicide enthusiast does not back down on his word... Also, in return, if you don't mind..."

I knew this was coming.

"What do you want? I'm not giving you a raise or easier work, if that's what you're after."

"Oh, it's nothing that extravagant. It's just, well, something piqued my interest a little earlier..."

Dazai steadily gazes in the driver's direction, his eyes brimming with curiosity.

"...Let me drive."

⬡ ⬡ ⬡

"AHHHHHHHHHHH!"

"Mwa-ha-ha-ha-ha-haaa! I am the wind!!"

"Wai— D-Dazai, stop the car! Stop the car this inst— Aaargh!"

"GAAAAAAH!!"

"Blerrrgh..."

⬡ ⬡ ⬡

"Ta-daa! Here we are, safe and sound!"

"Never again... I'm never going to let you drive...ever again...!"

Dazai gallantly leaps out of the taxi as the door opens, while I stumble and almost fall on my face. The driver, on the other hand, is passed out in the passenger seat. He's not getting up until morning, that's for sure.

"Wait. Are you carsick? C'mon—pull yourself together."

I get the sudden urge to kill him.

Carsick is not the word for this. My legs are trembling so much that I can't even stand. I have no sense of balance. I feel like some newborn herbivorous creature trying to stand on its own four wobbly legs for the first time. Not even the most rigorous martial arts training ever left me this exhausted.

"All right, then! Let's get to work! I'm going to start taking things seriously just like I promised!"

There's no way I could ask to rest now after the earful I gave him.

"The building mentioned in the e-mail is just up ahead... By the way, Kunikida, are you afraid of ghosts?"

"Ghosts? ...Do you really think someone afraid of ghosts can work at the Armed Detective Agency? Guns and knives are much more of a threat than some mystical apparition."

"Good. Because that's apparently where we're investigating."

I turn to see what he's pointing at, and I see a dilapidated black building standing in the bosom of the mountains. An abandoned hospital reeking of death and rot, shrouded in darkness, awaits us.

⬡ ⬡ ⬡

Why?

Why did we have to come here in the middle of the night? And on a night like this?

All living people fall ill. Just as there is no perfect mind, there is no perfect body. One would have to look no further than a hospital for proof. Everyone is born and dies in a hospital. One could say that hospitals act as the boundary between this world and the next—the dividing line between life and death. And a forgotten, decaying hospital is all the eerier.

Moonlight creeps in through the shattered windows, casting sapphire shadows of subtle grace over the rubble. Stagnant violet puddles resembling blood cover the floor, and out front are a bunch of spider lilies, their flowers a noxious shade of crimson.

"It's dark... I can hardly see a thing."

"But isn't that half the fun?"

As I drag my feet along the abandoned hospital's hallway floor, Dazai casually skips past me. The rotten walls are crumbling while old wires dangle from the ceiling. The window frames are missing, most of the equipment has been stolen, and the hospital's rooms are now nothing more than homes for insects. Who would ever willingly come to a place like this?

"The client requests that we find the source of the light and noise coming from somewhere here every night. There's no telling what might happen, so don't let your guard down."

"Sure... But, Kunikida, don't you think you're being a little too cautious?"

I glare at Dazai. "Only a fool underestimates the enemy. Being a member of our agency means to always expect the worst and act accordingly."

Lowering my center of gravity just to be even more careful, I prepare for a surprise attack while advancing down the hall.

"Are you scared?"

"I-I'm n-n-not scared, you idiot!"

"Then let's hurry up and get this over with."

"Don't be stupid. In movies like this, the first characters to get themselves killed are the careless ones who get carried away and run up ahead."

"And what kind of movie are we in?"

"Just shut up and take the lead. I'll keep an eye on the rear."

"Are you only saying that because you don't want to be in the—? Oh, wait. You said it was because it was too dark to see anything. Have you considered using a flashlight or something?"

I have. In fact, I would love to be able to have some light, but...

"If there really is somebody here, they're most likely going to run away if they see our lights. We're going to have to rely on the moonlight to get by."

"If you say so."

We travel through the darkness. The building creaks against the strong winds. I hear the sound of water dripping. Not only are there no private houses around this hospital, there aren't any buildings at all. Only the hills and vast woods watch over us as the pitch-black trees howl in the blustering wind.

I think back to the client's e-mail. "Neighboring residents"? There isn't a place fit to live for miles from here. The only nearby inhabitants are foxes and bears.

—*So just who is this client?*

—*Why wasn't there a name?*

—*Perhaps the client really is a vengeful spirit?*

Dazai's words spring to mind.

Nothing but darkness in every single direction. The howling wind blowing through the building's cracks is reminiscent of a woman's sobs.

....

I don't believe in ghosts. I teach algebra, and I'm a believer in the sciences. Vengeful spirits appearing to kill the living is nothing more than a delusion created by a fear of the dark—the unknown.

....

I'm not afraid, I'm not shaking, and I'm not crying, either!

"Ghost!!"

Gyaaah!!

Dazai's sudden shrieking from up ahead causes my heart to skip a beat. He turns around, staring at me with his mouth opened wide. Then, after getting a good look at me, he slowly but surely begins to grin.

That bastard...!

"I'm going to fire you for that!"

"Aw c'mon, you just looked so nervous that I wanted to take your mind off things."

"Go to hell!"

I hurry ahead and push past him. Damn it. It's dark. I can't see a thing. Eyes peering from the shadows, sighing coming from empty space: It's so dark that my mind's starting to play tricks on me.

Dark.

So dark.

I can't take it anymore.

"The Matchless Poet: Flashliiight!!"

Let there be light.

◇ ◇ ◇

After examining the inside of the abandoned hospital, it becomes clear that people have been coming here. There are scuff marks on the floor from a cart of some sort, footprints left from leather shoes, and threads from clothes. But it still isn't clear if this is evidence left by someone who sneaks in here every night or just the remnants of past lootings. I illuminate my surroundings with the flashlight I created, but it's not enough to eliminate the overpowering darkness and its hold over the hospital.

I am quite literally groping in the dark. The ocean of nothingness engulfs my feet as I light up the path before me, but casting the flashlight across my feet only throws the path forward into shadow. I timidly move forward, yet I still find nothing of importance.

"Looks like someone was just playing a prank. C'mon, let's head home," Dazai says as he turns on his heel, finally weary of this.

"Hold on. What happened to 'carefully and thoroughly investigating, examining, and reaching logical deductions'? Calling it quits already? We need to find more evidence bef—"

"That won't be necessary. Here, check this out."

He picks up a black cord with both ends disappearing into the floor... *Wait.*

"Is that...an electrical wire?"

And a rather new one, at that. It's obviously different from the interior wiring originally used in this old run-down hospital. This wire must have been installed within the past few months.

"We'll just follow this wire, and..."

Dazai draws in the wire while following it to its source. It was cleverly hidden, but we eventually find what's at the other end. He lifts it up.

"Hmm... Looks like a movie camera. Somebody must have secretly installed it here, and I bet this isn't the only one. Clearly, the client sent us a fake job offer so he could get you here and film you crying because you're afraid of ghosts. What a nasty person."

"I-I'm not crying!"

"You're right—only a baby would be afraid of a dark building."

"......"

"Besides, a spirit haunting a hospital wouldn't be so gutsy. They died of an illness, right? I mean, if some kind of accident did them in, then they'd be haunting wherever it happened, after all. A ghost who died from illness wouldn't have the courage to kill anyone. At the very worst, they'd just be filled with regret. Their line would be something like 'I didn't wanna diiie.' Can you believe it, though? The lucky dog died, and here they are complaining!"

"Dazai... Hey... Th-that's enough..."

You're gonna piss off a vengeful spirit.

"Like, if there's gonna be an angry ghost, then it needs to be a skinny woman who died from pulmonary tuberculosis—all skin and bones, y'know? And she's gotta have wet, disheveled hair covering her face and say something like 'It's not fair. Why do you get to live and not me? Save me from the grip of this dark-nessss! Save me from this paaain! Ah, it hurts! My blood, my bones, my flesh, my entrails...! Raaahhh!!'"

"Heeeeeelp!!"

At the sudden high-pitched scream, my heart jumps into my throat and nearly out of my mouth, too. But not a moment later, as I'm drenched in a cold sweat, I realize:

That scream came from a living person.

"Did you hear that...?"

"It came from over there! Follow me!"

Unable to wait for Dazai, I dash down the rotting hall, rush down the staircase as quickly as possible, then race down the hallway, kicking up gravel all the while. Following the direction of the scream, I end up in the basement.

The ceiling is falling apart, just like the deteriorating walls. The boiler room, medicine room, radiography room, and the morgue run along the hallway. Following the voice, I plunge into the old boiler room.

I found her!

A woman's right hand swiftly emerges out of the large water tank, struggling desperately. I race over and peer inside to find a young woman submerged, dressed in only her underwear. Her opposite arm is cuffed to a handle at the bottom to keep her from getting out. She's going to drown if I don't do something!

"The hell—?!"

"We have to get these off!" Dazai shouts as he grabs on to some iron bars. They lie across the top of the water tank normally used for laundry, preventing the woman from escaping. I grab the bars with both hands and pull with everything I've got, but they hardly even budge, as if there is some sort of lock. My eyes meet her dark-brown ones, opened as wide as could be. They hopelessly plead with mine: *Help me.*

"We're going to save you! Move closer to the edge of the tank!"

I wave my hand, instructing her to move. She presses her back against the wall and curls her body as if she got the message. Then I take out the gun strapped to my waist, remove the safety, and aim it at the water tank's outer wall.

"Get back, Dazai!"

I angle the pistol in a way so that no bullets would ricochet and hit the woman inside. After that, I shoot three bullets into the outside wall, piercing and cracking the tank. Water spews out.

Facing the fissures, I spin into an ax kick. The momentum buries my heel into the earthenware and mortar outer wall, shattering it with a single strike. Gallons of water instantly escape from the large hole.

"Cough... Cough, cough!"

She ravenously gasps for air after the water finally drains enough to expose her face. It looks like we made it in time. Dazai rotates the large faucet handle, shutting off the water supply.

"Are you okay?"

I reach through the iron bars, offering a handkerchief. Her fingers tremble as she grabs it.

"Someone tried to drown you... Did you see who it was?" Dazai asks. After a fit of coughing, the victim finally speaks up, still breathing heavily.

"I was...kidnapped. I was visiting Yokohama on business one day until I suddenly lost consciousness... Next thing I knew, I was here."

Dazai and I exchange glances.

○ ○ ○

With Dazai's help, we break the iron bars and remove her hand-cuffs to complete the rescue. The bars were triple locked with cylinder locks, so I had no choice but to use the butt of my gun to break them.

"My name is Nobuko Sasaki. I teach at a university in Tokyo. I was visiting Yokohama and suddenly lost consciousness...and when I woke up, I was here."

Even while pale and dripping wet, Miss Sasaki courageously explains what happened to her.

"Miss Sasaki, do you know how many days ago you were kidnapped?"

"I apologize... I can't say for sure, since I was unconscious for so long... However, judging by how I feel and how hungry I am, I would say it hasn't been any longer than two or three days..."

The first victim in the Yokohama missing-persons case disappeared thirty-five days ago, and the eleventh victim, seven. If her assumption is correct, then there is a high possibility she's a victim we didn't know about.

"............"

Deep in thought, Dazai keeps silent with his arms crossed.

Miss Sasaki is a slightly thin woman with long black hair. She appears to be around the same age as me. She's trembling, and understandably so. The kidnapper must have stripped her of everything but her underwear. Aside from Dazai's overcoat, she's nearly naked and soaking wet in the middle of the night.

Her hands tightly wrapped around her elbows and her legs stretched out on the floor are especially delicate. The clothes clinging to her body sketch the outline of an alluring figure. I feel almost as if I could see through her remarkably fine porcelain skin. Wet hair clings to her nape as water drips onto her chest. I avert my gaze for absolutely no reason.

"More importantly, there are others trapped here, too! I heard them screaming."

"What?!"

The other missing people are here, too? Were they being kept prisoner in this building after being kidnapped as well?

"I'll take you to them! Follow me." The woman staggers to her feet and turns around.

But...

"...Wait." I place a hand on Miss Sasaki's shoulder, stopping her. "Dazai, what do you think?"

"The way she's dressed makes me feel things," he says with a straight face.

"Be serious!"

"...Her story's too good to be true," Dazai replies, this time crossing his arms. "It's just too convenient. We came here to investigate a mysterious light and strange voices, and we just happen to find a victim from the missing-persons case? These two cases are separate, completely unrelated, except for the fact that they're *our* cases... Miss Sasaki, when was the last time you saw the criminal?"

"I'm sorry, but I never actually saw anyone. When I woke up, the tank was already being filled with water, almost covering my face. I suspect the kidnapper turned on the faucet and left five or so minutes before I woke up."

That must have been when she screamed. What unbelievable timing.

"Then that'd mean the criminal was here up until a few moments ago, and I highly doubt they didn't notice us coming. So the question is: Why'd they do it?"

"Perhaps they heard us coming, so they panicked. Or perhaps..."
It's all an elaborate trap.

But for us to run away in fear of a trap is out of the question. If there's a high chance the other missing people are here, then there's no way we can turn back now.

"Thirty-five days have already passed since the first victim was kidnapped. If they're being kept here, then they don't have much longer. Dazai, I want you to keep her safe and follow me." I walk down the hallway, my gun in hand.

After contacting the city police just in case, we follow Miss Sasaki until she guides us to the morgue. Corpses are quite valuable, so the doors are sturdier than normal to protect from theft. The iron door is latched shut. It's the perfect place to confine someone. I make sure it's not booby-trapped before breaking the lock and rushing into the room.

With one hand over the other, I point the gun and flashlight forward. Wall to wall, the morgue is around thirty-five feet long and dreadfully dark. The room is almost completely bare, most everything having been moved or stolen. All that's left are a stretcher with bent legs, a ripped body bag, and the lockers on the walls. Nothing else. Nobody dead or alive... Wait.

Something in the back of the room moved in reaction to the light. I shine my flashlight in its direction.

"Hel...p...us..."

The room isn't empty. There are four people bunched in an iron cage against the wall, wearing only their underwear, just like Miss Sasaki.

"Where am I?"

"I heard a woman scream... What's going on?"

"There's no need to worry. We're here to save you. We already saved the woman you heard screaming. Is anyone hurt?"

"N-no, we're fine. But where are we? And why are we here?"

I get closer. Attached to the wall opposite the entrance is a metal cage made to transport wild animals. It would be hard to unfasten with the tools I have in hand. The cage's structure itself is simple but extremely strong. Undoubtedly, much time would be needed to break it open.

"Hmm... An electronic lock, huh?" Dazai approaches the lock for further inspection. "Is it password protected? Or maybe biometric authentication? Or maybe it's voice controlled? ...'Open sesame'! 'Flash and thunder'! 'Mine has been a life of much shame'! Hmm... That didn't work. Guess we'll just have to break it open."

What on earth was that last line?

"If we want to break it, we'll probably have to start with this—"

The moment Dazai goes to touch the lock pad, Miss Sasaki lets out a piercing scream.

"Don't touch the lock!"

Dazai turns around in astonishment. A red light flashes on the lock pad. The sound of metal dropping echoes from the floor above, and I hear something opening. Milky-white gas shoots into the cage. After I instinctively rush over, my eyes and throat violently burn with lancinating pain. The caged victims let out bloodcurdling screams.

"It's poison gas!!"

The extreme pain causes tears to well in my eyes. I can hardly see a thing. It's all a blur, as if everything is dancing before me. I may have accidentally breathed in some of the gas, but that doesn't mean I can abandon these people. I place a hand on the cage.

"Get back! It's too late!"

Somebody grabs me by the arm and pulls me back.

Don't you dare tell me what I can and can't do. I have to save them. The victims must not die. That's the ideal. That's the way the world should be.

"Kunikida, hurry!" Dazai yells to me from behind.

No. This isn't right.

"No!" Miss Sasaki wraps me in her arms, stopping me.

Why? Why are you holding me back? Nobody deserves to die. I won't let them.

Dazai drags me out of the room. All I remember is screaming something.

All four victims are dead.

CHAPTER II

11th

Returning home late, I face my inkstone in silence.

Though this is a day I will never forget, I will not inscribe it in my notebook.

No matter how difficult the trial, no matter how great my disgrace, I must laugh.

But for now, there is only silence.

I read the paper at my desk at the office. The news has been chaotic all morning. Sensational reports flood the television and Internet.

MISSING YOKOHAMA VISITORS FOUND DEAD

DID A PRIVATE DETECTIVE AGENCY'S MEDDLING LEAD TO THE VICTIMS' DEATHS?

And then there are the images—the white gas, the suffering victims, and me, grabbing on to the cage. It's only a matter of time before the pictures make the front page of the newspaper. The agency's phone has been ringing off the hook all morning with no end in sight. So far, they've all been complaints, but it won't be long before the victims' families begin to call us to threaten legal action. To make matters worse, we still have no leads as to where the remaining seven missing persons are.

Who took the pictures the moment the victims were killed, and why make them public?

The phone on my desk gives a teeth-grinding trill. I reach for the receiver, but Dazai promptly snatches it up and puts it back in its cradle. The ringing stops.

"Looks like this is exactly what the enemy wanted, huh?" Dazai says cheerfully. He's carrying a photo in his hand. "If it's any consolation, this is a really good picture of you."

I silently try to take it from him, but he nimbly lifts his arm into the air before I can.

"Why don't you take the rest of the day off? You look awful."

"…No. There's work to be done."

"Wow. You're not gonna take a day off even after all this? You know, someone threw a rock at me on two separate occasions while I was trying to come into the office today."

I look outside. A few protesters have been standing in front of the agency, causing a ruckus since morning. There will undoubtedly be even more tomorrow.

"'Take a day off'? Have you lost your mind? We have a mission of utmost priority: *Find the criminal behind this.*"

"Well… Yeah. You're right," Dazai agrees with a blank look on his face.

"Where's Miss Sasaki?"

"She's in the infirmary getting examined by Dr. Yosano. Sounds like she's gonna be okay."

"Let's pay her a little visit."

I get out of my chair. Miss Sasaki is the only known victim to have had contact with the murderer and lived to tell the tale. We can probably figure out who the perpetrator is if we can learn how they're kidnapping everyone.

I casually look down at the picture before following Dazai into the infirmary. You can clearly see my face in the pictures along with Miss Sasaki's and the victims', but the most of Dazai you can see is the tail of his overcoat. How was he able to avoid the secret photos?

O O O

"I'm sorry... I really wish I could help you, but..."

Miss Sasaki helplessly gazes at the floor.

"I've always been prone to illness, and I'm anemic, which causes me to faint every now and then. I was feeling especially ill the day I was abducted... I passed out at the train station, probably from the anemia."

In that case, I guess she wouldn't have any idea how she was abducted. However...

"Then that would mean someone abducted you in the midst of the confusion after you passed out."

Kidnapping someone in the middle of a place as crowded as Yokohama Station would be impossible. Carrying an unconscious woman would draw even more attention. Either there are multiple kidnappers or someone's using a very clever trick...

"Let me just say...thank you so much for saving me yesterday. I... I don't have any friends or family to turn to, so..."

Miss Sasaki hangs her head low in silence. She doesn't say another word after that. With her naturally delicate features coupled together with the porcelain skin, she reminds me of a marionette doll whose strings have been cut. Actually, her own experience isn't too much different. As if her thread of life had been cut, she was almost killed by an unidentified serial killer for who knows why, and her life could still very well be in danger.

"You even allowed me to stay at your home last night..."

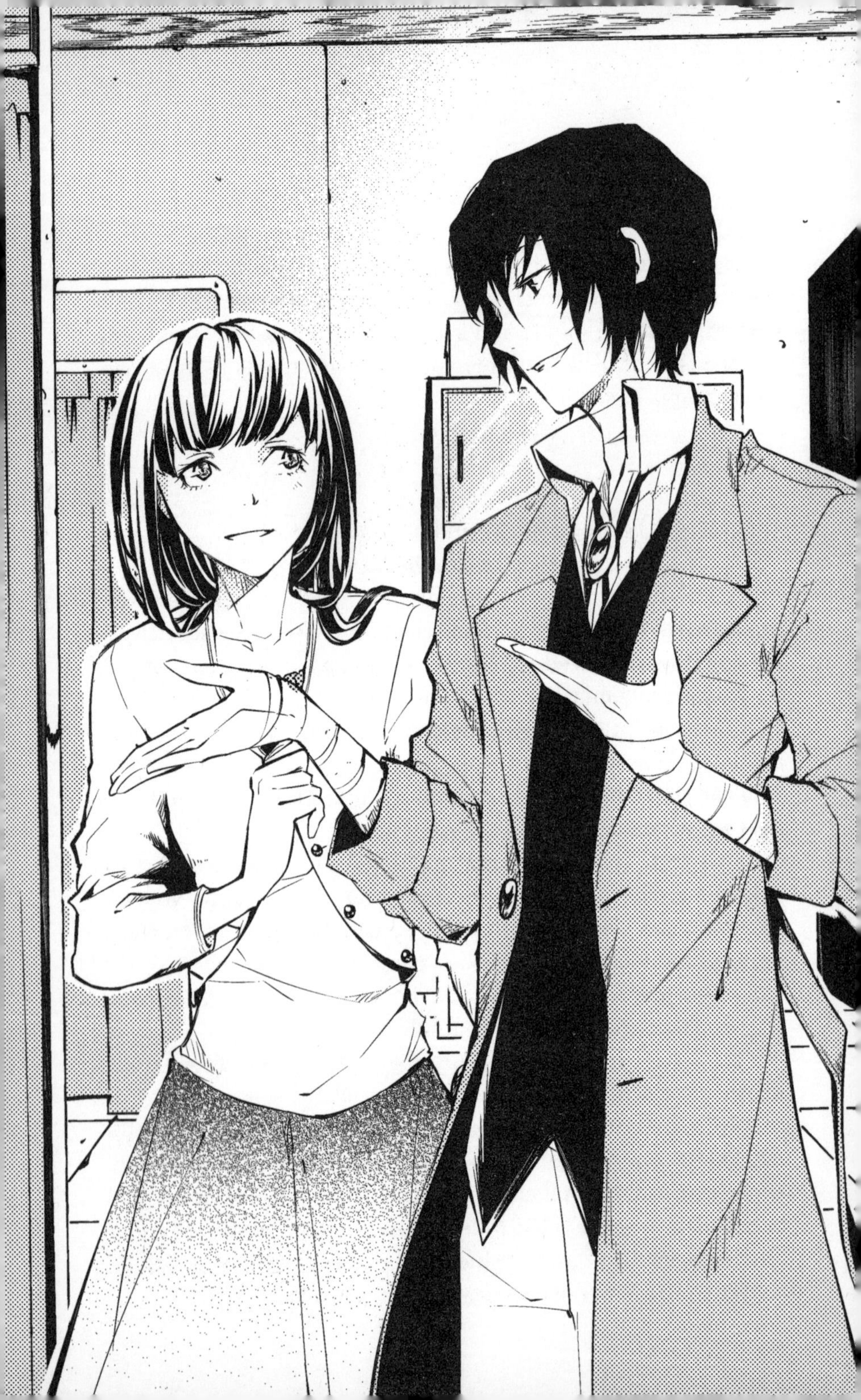

......*Hmm?*

"Hold on. Where did you stay last night?"

"My place," Dazai nonchalantly replies.

....

............Are things like this the norm nowadays?

"Thank you so much, Mr. Dazai. You... You were very...kind to me last night..."

Miss Sasaki flushes bashfully for some reason.

"What's wrong, Kunikida? You've got a really weird look on your face."

"Dazai... Don't you think that's taking things a little too fast?"

"I... I was the one who asked him to let me stay over. I basically forced him."

"Hey, don't worry about it. I simply did what any gentleman would. Besides, I'm used to getting asked for things from people I've just met," he replies with a smile.

....

I have no interest in frivolous love affairs. Two people must have mutual respect for each other when building a relationship. If you ask me, an unplanned single night of fleeting passion is unforgivable and shameless. So—therefore—for this reason alone, it doesn't matter how popular a fool like Dazai may be, because I am not the least bit jealous or frustrated.

Not the least bit jealous!

◇ ◇ ◇

"What a beautiful, misfortunate woman," Dazai says with a smirk. We've returned to the office to prepare for our next investigation.

"So that's your type?"

"I like all types of women. They're the bearers of all human life, a source of mystery. But I do like the fact that Miss Sasaki would probably kill herself with me if I asked."

"Go marry a cicada or something, then."

Relations between the sexes must be pure and strong. The only feminine company I intend to keep will be with my ideal spouse, where we complement and lift each other up, and I will be with her until the day I draw my last breath. That is my *ideal*. It's also written in my notebook.

"What about you, Kunikida? What do you think of Miss Sasaki?"

"She's a victim and a witness to the case. That's all."

"I'm asking only because I can't even begin to imagine, but... what's your ideal woman like?"

"You're free to read about it."

I open my notebook to the page titled "Spouse" and show him. All my future plans are written here.

"What is this, an encyclopedia?!"

His expression slowly hardens as he skims over the page.

"...Whoa. Oh no, no, no... This is just... Wow. I'm..."

"The hell kind of reaction is that? Is it weird?"

"No, not at all. I think all guys can relate to the ideals...of each section."

"Right? What's wrong with having standards?"

"Exactly. I agree with you one hundred percent, Kunikida. A word of advice, though: Never show this to a woman. It'd really turn them off. I mean, even I'm struggling to keep myself from yelling 'A girl like this doesn't exist!'"

Is it really that far-fetched?

"Okay, I get it. Now let's get to work and find that kidnapper. By the way, have you found out anything else?"

"There's one thing I noticed."

"What's that?"

"If you truly wish to pursue your ideal woman, then we're going to have to do something about those boring glasses first."

Dazai swiftly swipes the glasses off my face, then puts them on. They look awful on him.

"Enough! Give those back!"

So long as my work isn't hindered, then nothing else matters. Besides, simply wearing nice glasses isn't going to magically improve my life. And Dazai looks even more comical with them on... Even more ridiculous than usual for some odd reason.

"......Glasses?"

Glasses. The photos of the victims. Their faces. The monitoring equipment. The hotel they stayed in—

"Something the matter, Kunikida?"

The missing people all left the hotel of their own accord, and they all stayed in Yokohama alone. So that means the security footage of everyone entering and leaving the hotel is...

"Come on, Dazai. We're leaving."

I snatch my glasses and put them back on.

"I figured out who the kidnapper is."

○ ○ ○

The ocean breeze soars past the Port of Yokohama. Dazai and I stand on the levee at the mouth by the shore. I gaze into the sky. The sun is already high, peeking through the sea of clouds and shining onto us. I do not feel as fine as the weather, however. A familiar taxi stops before me.

"Detective Kunikida! Please get in."

A familiar cabdriver waves me over, and we waste no time climbing in.

"I apologize for the sudden call."

"Oh, don't be. I would go through fire and water for you and the agency, Detective! So are you in a hurry to get somewhere? Don't you worry! The speed limit means nothing to me!"

"It should. Anyway, do you remember the missing-persons case we spoke of last evening? Well, I figured out who the kidnapper is."

"What?! I saw the news about the abandoned hospital. I feel so sorry for those poor victims... So we're going to arrest the kidnapper, yes? Roger that! We have to hurry, though, or he'll get away. So where is this perpetrator?"

"Right here."

"Excuse me?"

"You're the kidnapper, and inside this taxi is where the kidnappings have been taking place."

"Uh... I don't think I'm following you, Detective. What are you saying?"

"I thought, 'Who would be able to kidnap someone in this city without anyone noticing? Where in Yokohama would a victim be comfortable alone with a complete stranger?' The answer is here. You used sleeping gas on the victims, then kidnapped them. While wearing a gas mask yourself, of course."

"Wait... No, no, no. Hold on. I'm pretty sure the investigation indicated that the victims all left of their own accord, by themselves, and mysteriously disappeared. I heard there were no records of them ever getting into any vehicle or going inside any building. If all the victims got into this taxi, then wouldn't there be a record of a phone call or of them hailing a cab?"

"Yes, there would be. And that's why there is no doubt in my mind that every victim got into this taxi. Of course, the city police weren't able to find any records no matter how hard they looked. Why? Because they were looking at the wrong date. The victims didn't get in this taxi on the day they went missing."

"What... What are you trying to say?"

"Okay, Kunikida, we're not going to get anywhere trying to answer each and every one of his questions. Let me explain exactly what happened," Dazai chimes in. "Driver, you were searching for certain customers during your daily work shift. The conditions for a target were simple: They had to be in Yokohama alone and heading to their hotel, they had to be wearing something that partially covered their face such as a hat, glasses, or sunglasses, and they had to be around the same height as you. You have a small frame, which is why women would be viable candidates as long as they met those few requirements. All of this would make it appear as if you had no relation to the victim, and you could disrupt the investigation."

"I... I'm afraid I don't follow. I—"

"Yes, yes. Let me finish first, okay? You're a taxi driver who operates in the area. Those requirements may be strict, but you'd be able to find someone who matched them in two, three days tops. Then, when just the right person happened to show up, you used sleeping gas on them just like Kunikida mentioned. After that, you went to a secret hideout, held the victims prisoner there, and stole their clothes and belongings. That's why the victims at the abandoned hospital were in their underwear. Now this is where you really begin to shine." Dazai claps his hands giddily before continuing. "Next, you dressed in the victim's clothing and *disguised yourself as them*. After that, it's just as you told us last night. All you have to do is put on a little makeup, stuff your cheeks and clothing a bit, and you're someone else. Of course, you must have religiously practiced and chosen only people you were confident you could pull off, though. Plus, you weren't trying to deceive *people*, only video footage. You went to the hotel the victims planned to stay at and *purposely made sure* the security cameras saw you."

I think back to the footage I viewed during the investigation. In hindsight, there was an unnaturally high rate of people with their face covered—six in glasses and two in sunglasses. The remaining three had either a hat or long hair, leaving only a portion of their face exposed to the security cameras. This was possible only because he selected victims wearing specific clothing that would be easy to emulate.

"The rest is simple. You leave the victims' belongings in the hotel room and check out the next morning in broad daylight.

By leaving a record of what appears to be the victim entering, checking in, and exiting the hotel, the police would stubbornly focus on investigating what happened to the victim after they left. Naturally, they didn't find anything, though, since you undoubtedly know Yokohama inside and out. At the very least, you knew where you would be recorded and where you could escape to avoid any security cameras. That's why the more we investigated, the more it appeared as if the victims intentionally spirited themselves away while making sure there would be no records of it."

"This is absurd. This hypothetical, purely speculative situation you're proposing is—is nothing without…without evidence. That's right—you've got no evidence to support your claim."

"I wouldn't be so sure of that. You would have been more than able to conduct Miss Sasaki's kidnapping on your own as well," I continue explaining from where Dazai left off. "Abducting Miss Sasaki after she passed out at the station must have been your easiest job yet. I'll bet you felt like the luckiest man alive. People usually call an ambulance if they see somebody suddenly faint, but it takes time for the ambulances to arrive from the hospital. But there's always a taxi waiting in front of the station for passengers, and luckily for Miss Sasaki, a Good Samaritan happened to be present to save her. This well-intentioned individual wanted to get her to the hospital as quickly as possible, so he decided to have a taxi take her. That's when you took her away, bold as brass, except you didn't take her to the hospital like you were supposed to."

"I…"

The driver sounds as if he wants to say something, but he doesn't speak another word. I can't see his expression clearly from where we're sitting, either. I shift my gaze to the interior of the car, where I find a few small white particles in one of the crevices. I pinch what I can with my fingertips.

"If you're going to turn yourself in, you should probably do it quickly. It won't be long until we have evidence. I'm sure you cleaned the inside of this car, but there's still some residue from the gas. A lab analysis will confirm it in no time."

"I... I have no idea where that came from. It must have been from one of my customers. That doesn't count as evidence."

The driver barely manages to stammer out the words. Nevertheless, he admitted his guilt the moment he started making excuses.

"Evidence isn't even necessary to prove you're the only one who could have done it." I begin to lay out the basis of the argument. "The only way to use the trick Dazai mentioned would be to get the victims into a taxi, and you had two of the victims in your vehicle, which is no different from admitting you gave rides to the other nine."

"That isn't physical evidence, Detective Kunikida," the driver plainly states while avoiding eye contact. "Everything you've presented has been circumstantial evidence. It's not as if you found a weapon in my house or have video evidence of me committing a crime. Sure, you could file charges, but I wouldn't be convicted."

It's my turn to fall silent. He's right. We would need physical evidence to connect him to the victims: blood, fingerprints, video recordings, a confession with information only the criminal would know...

We don't have the necessary hard evidence. In fact, our case could be dismissed due to a lack of probable cause as things stand now. From the way the driver's talking, it sounds like he made sure to dispose of all the physical evidence. He's cleverer than I thought. What's my next move?

But what he says next completely disproves my assumptions.

"Detective Kunikida... Let's make a deal. If you accept my conditions, I will turn myself in."

"What?"

"I would like the Armed Detective Agency to protect me and

guarantee my safety in return for my confession. I request only seventy-two hours of your time until I receive witness protection following the prosecutorial investigation."

"A witness protection deal? What are you talking about?"

"There's no time... I'm going to be killed. They're going to kill me."

"Wait. I'm not following. Tell me step-by-step what's going on. Who's going to kill you? And for what?!"

"I wish I never did business with that lot... I should have never tried to get into the organ-trafficking business alone! And now I've made them angry! This is bad... This is really bad. I can't get in touch with any of the buyers, either. They've cut me loose! But why? They were never supposed to find out... But they're already onto me. And they're getting closer..."

"I see. So that's what's going on here."

Dazai places a hand on his chin and nods.

"Dazai, what's going on?! What is he rambling about?!"

"It's exactly how it sounds. He was selling the victims to an organ-trafficking syndicate, but the month's supply rose too high relative to demand. Naturally, this led to a drop in prices, throwing the market into confusion. Imagine a private one-man business suddenly entering a supply market more or less controlled by a large corporation. How would the large corporation feel?"

"They would get mad, I guess?"

"It would be healthy competition if these were normal, legal companies. But these organ-trafficking businesses are run by underground groups who profit off blood and violence. Causing trouble on their turf would only anger—"

The next moment, the car is suddenly hit, then hit again so hard its wheels leave the ground. A high-pitched echo follows. The taxi's right side lifts into the air as the windows shatter along with the sound of gunshots.

"We're under fire! Get down!" I yell out.

The car rocks back and forth as if being pummeled with a hammer, and shards of glass rain down inside.

"It's them! H-help, help me... I don't wanna die!"

"Hey! Wait!"

The driver opens the car door before bolting in the opposite direction of the gunfire.

"Kunikida, we have to catch him before the enemy does, or we'll never know what really happened! We can't let him escape or turn up dead in a grove somewhere!" Dazai shouts, keeping his head down. That's easier said than done, though! "Okay, I'll go after the driver! You distract the enemies!"

"Dazai, wait! It's too dangerous to go alone!"

Dazai darts out of the car without even listening to my warning. I can't allow a rookie to go off on his own during his first shoot-out. We don't have any other options, though. I curse to myself while getting a look at the enemy. Three men stand dressed in black suits and black sunglasses, equipped with submachine guns smuggled in from abroad via the black market. Judging from their attire, their skills, and their ruthless willingness to suddenly turn the place into a war zone, it's clear who they are...

"Damn it! This couldn't be any worse... It's the **Port Mafia!**"

The Port Mafia is an underground organization that uses the Port of Yokohama as their base of operations. They're the cruelest, most coldhearted criminal syndicate in the city, willing to follow any orders from their boss and crush all who oppose them. The three men here are from that organization. The longer this goes on, the more they have the advantage.

"**The Matchless Poet:** Stun Grenade!"

I record the word in my notebook before tearing it out. The sheet of paper twists into a grenade the size of my fist. Aiming at the group, I hurl the grenade out the broken window. Stun grenades are nonlethal sonic weapons used to temporarily disorient an enemy's senses. It blows up right in front of them, emitting a light so bright and creating an explosion so thunderous that it could give a sick man a heart attack. They fall to their knees while covering their temples, perhaps completely taken by surprise at being countered with a flashbang. I use this momentary distraction to leap out of the taxi and charge the enemies. I elbow the man closest to me in the neck, knocking him to the ground. I keep my elbow out and charge the next criminal, following up with a high kick to the face. The last armed man tries to hit me with his gun, but I swerve to the side, evading the strike. As he staggers off-balance, I grab his wrist and twist while pulling inside. Then I throw him into the air with a four-corner throw. The Mafia member goes flying and lands cranium first, immediately losing consciousness.

"Good grief."

After making sure they're all out, I walk back to the taxi.

I really hope Dazai's all right...

Just then, I suddenly sense an ever-increasing thirst for blood coming from behind. Something flies past my side before I can even turn around. The black torrent runs through right where I was just standing, hitting the taxi and *cutting right through it, too*. As the vehicle completely splits in half, springs and shafts take to the air, scattering every which way. Without even a moment to let my surprise sink in, I kick off the ground to evade. The nearby sign and handrails are finely sliced into pieces. After rolling across the ground and looking back, I see a small-framed man clad in black in the distance.

"*Cough, cough...*"

That must be the source of the bloodlust.

"*Cough...* I came thinking this was going to be an easy side job. I wasn't expecting to run into someone skilled enough to neutralize three men in the blink of an eye. I'm impressed. Now let's see how you fare against **Rashomon**."

With no weapon in hand, the young man simply walks toward me with his back hunched, occasionally coughing. However, the malice oozing from his body soon transforms into a silent but furious storm.

A man short of stature dressed in a black overcoat, with the skill to control a black torrent—the Port Mafia's Hellhound.

"You... You're **Ryuunosuke Akutagawa** from the Port Mafia, aren't you?"

"The one and only. I was sent here by the boss to dispose of the fool who trespassed on our turf. Where is he?"

"He's not here. He ran away with his tail tucked between his legs."

I point in the direction the driver ran, but my eyes remain locked on Akutagawa. I don't look away—not even for a second. This man is the worst of the worst. Even the toughest criminals run away in tears when they hear Akutagawa's despicable name. The Black-Fanged Hellhound, the Skill User of Destruction and Disaster, the Apostle of Calamity and Despair: There are too many aliases to count. This is my first time actually meeting him, but judging by what he did to the taxi, he's even more dangerous than the rumors made him out to be.

So what's my next move? It's simple. His target is the kidnapper, and there's no reason for me to risk my life to protect a kidnapper against someone this dangerous. All I need to do is back off.

"He's a witness. I cannot allow you to kill him until he tells us where the other missing people are. If you want to go after him, you're going to have to get past me first."

"You're willing to risk your life for a murderer? Just as I expected."

Damn it. I can't believe how stupid I can be. But as a member of the Armed Detective Agency, I cannot allow our witness to be helplessly killed by this scumbag.

Do what must be done. I mentally recite the phrase from my notebook. Akutagawa's black overcoat wriggles. It's as if a thousand specters gathered and meshed, taking form. It's no longer a

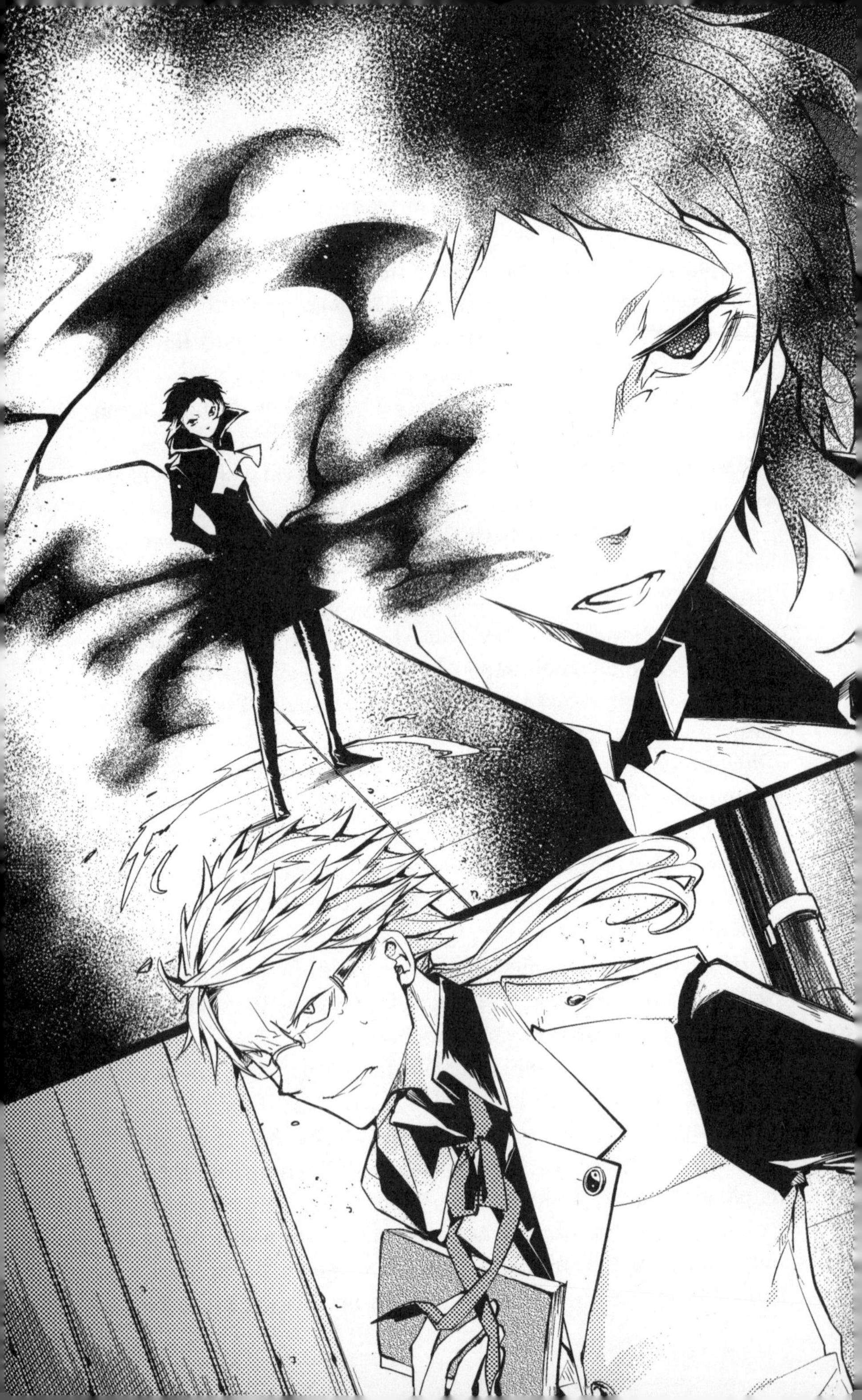

coat; part of it transforms into a claw, while another part begins to take the shape of a piercing fang.

"Ryuunosuke Akutagawa, the Port Mafia's attack dog."

"Doppo Kunikida, Armed Detective Agency."

Akutagawa launches a shadowy blade in one explosive motion. It disperses into a black rain, heading right in my direction. I jump to the side. A few dark blades pierce my shirt while the others stab the wall behind me, leaving numerous holes. I jot down a word in my notebook and tear out the sheet before he can draw his blade to attack. The piece of paper instantly transforms into a wire gun. Squeezing the trigger, I shoot the hook...but moments before the iron-penetrating hook reaches him, it's deflected by an invisible wall.

"What...?!"

I saw no signs of him moving to defend. Is this another one of his skills? Before I can even reel in my airborne hook, part of Akutagawa's coat transforms into a shadowy beast. With a roar, it swings its head. It's quick!

I twist away to dodge, but its fangs tear into my left shoulder. Blood spurts out of the wound, but I don't have time to stop the bleeding. I step back while evading the beast's relentless fangs. I have no chance to counter, let alone even get near the thing!

"Is running away the only thing you know how to do? You're putting me to sleep," he scoffs, still standing upright. A cold bead of sweat runs down my cheek. He's strong.

Akutagawa speedily shoots his lethal shadowy blade at me from only a few feet away, giving me no chance to do anything other than dodge. To make matters worse, any projectile I throw at him is easily knocked aside. Even if I do hit him, he's being protected by that mysterious force field. He has no openings.

I dodge the flurry of attacks until I land on a paved road, where a sudden unidentifiable chill eerily shoots down my spine.

A blade thrusts up from the pavement before shooting back into the air like a fountain of spears.

He was getting me to focus on the aerial attacks while he

used another blade to pierce the ground! I try to turn my body and jump away, but the ground is uneven, and I'm too late. The pitch-black blade penetrates my side and exits through my back.

"Gah...!"

My vision blurs from the excruciating pain, and I helplessly fall to my knees. This isn't good. The next attack is coming. If I stop moving for even a second, I'm dead...but there's nothing I can do. The black fabric of Rashomon wraps around my neck, lifting me off the ground. It bends like a serpent's neck, then catapults me into the nearby wall.

"Pathetic. I guess I shouldn't have expected much from a detective agency that works for chump change. Don't worry. It'll all be over when I snap your head off."

The black fabric tightens around my neck. I start to see red.

"There's always someone—someone who wants...to get in the way of my work!"

As Akutagawa's skill strangles me, I shoot my wire gun. My target isn't Akutagawa, though. The airborne iron wire's hook directly hits *the water pipe running up the building next to him*, showering him with water.

"What...?!"

He raises his arm to block, but the high-pressure stream fully drenches him and the ground around him.

"Fool. Do you really think a little water is going to scare me?"

I raise another sheet of paper in my left hand into the air with *something else I wrote down* while making the wire gun.

"The Matchless Poet: Stun Gun!"

I instantly turn on the handheld high-voltage stun gun before tossing it into the puddle of water. A flash of light shoots out, and sparks fly.

"Nnng—gaaah?!"

Using the water as a conductor, the submerged stun gun emits beams of violet and white light. A purple flash of lightning jolts through Akutagawa's wet body like a boa constrictor wrapping around its prey. The flash shines as bright as the sun before eventually disappearing along with the hiss of steam and the crack of the ground splitting under it. Rashomon's grip around my neck loosens, and I land on the pavement below. As I cradle my injured neck and side, I glare at Akutagawa. He's on his knees as steam and white smoke rise from his body.

"Heh-heh... Ah-ha-ha-ha!"

Akutagawa's shoulders shake as he laughs. He can still move after taking a shock like that?

"Looks like I was wrong about the Armed Detective Agency. Heh. This is wonderful. Truly wonderful."

"...Come at me if you want to keep going. I still have plenty more paper left." I force myself to my feet, then get back into stance with the wire gun.

"By all means, I would love the opportunity to see whether you have what it takes to kill me, but it seems we have guests."

I follow Akutagawa's gaze and see the city police approach with their sirens blazing. Somebody must have reported the gunshots.

"A pathetic traitor won't be able to hide for long before we hunt him down. I will withdraw for today. We'll continue this soon." He coughs and turns his back to me. He leaves just like that, with the same nonchalance as if he was going home after a walk. Honestly speaking, continuing to fight and withdrawing probably aren't too different from his point of view.

"I'd rather you not come back..."

I fall to my knees while watching him walk away. Akutagawa from the Port Mafia is just as— No, he's even fiercer than the rumors say. No thanks on the rematch. For now, I just want to go home and sleep like the dead.

⬡ ⬡ ⬡

Unfortunately, this is no time for a nap. After a short break, I return to the agency to report what happened. In the company's infirmary, I have my stomach wound temporarily patched up, then head to the office. That's where I find Dazai sipping on some tea as if he was relaxing after a hard day's work.

"Dazai, you caught the taxi driver, right?"

"Of course. I tied him right up and handed him off to the police. He was actually thrilled that the Mafia wouldn't be able to assassinate him anymore."

I'm relieved. It appears Dazai isn't as stupid as I originally thought. I was almost worried that he knew it was the Mafia attacking us and used chasing the kidnapper as an excuse to escape. Nevertheless, everything ended up working out, so I guess it was just a groundless fear.

"It looks like the taxi driver will be charged for the series of kidnappings. Case closed."

I worked my fingers to the bone on this case, and in return, I get paid nothing. The military police will toss us a letter of thanks and a small gift as an expression of their gratitude, and that will be the end of it. Good grief.

"I don't feel like working anymore. Let's get today's tasks over with and go out for a drink."

"Your treat?" Dazai asks, beaming with joy.

"You're a real piece of work. I'll pay, but you better work your ass off tomorrow."

I return to my desk and take care of my remaining duties. I skim through some documents that are being passed around, then make a few business calls. After that, I start recording the case's details until inadvertently glancing at my work computer and noticing I got an e-mail. Paying little attention, I begin to follow the sentences with my eyes. After finishing the e-mail, I start over from the beginning.

"Dazai."

The moment I call for him is the moment I realize I've been holding my breath.

"We'll have to take a rain check on those drinks. We've got work to do."

"Whaaat? But I was all ready to drink. There's a hole in my stomach shaped exactly like a cup of sake."

"We got a job offer...from the anonymous client who lured us into the abandoned hospital."

My throat is dry, and my tongue is stuck in place. The next words don't want to come out.

"It's a request to defuse a bomb. If we don't find and defuse it by sundown tomorrow, *over one hundred people will die.*"

INTERLUDE I

It's the middle of the night. On the busy downtown street, a man gazes at the flickering lights in silence from the car window. He's parked on the side of the quiet road, not another soul in sight. The diodes in the car faintly illuminate his face.

"I can't wait until this job is over," he mutters to himself while typing on the thin laptop on his knees. Strings of letters cover the entire screen.

"I mean, I'm not good at this electronic stuff."

He smiles faintly, his fingertips nimbly tapping the keyboard. The letters dance across the surface.

"...But I guess this isn't something I can let others do." He chuckles to himself in the dim car.

"Now, will the detective agency—will Kunikida—be able to see through the smoke and mirrors and save the city of Yokohama?"

The man—Dazai—looks out the car window. The flickering city lights of Yokohama ripple over the dark billowing sea.

CHAPTER III

12th

Here at the office, the midnight oil burns until morning.

I sit before a solitary light, unable to sleep most of the evening.

The countless deaths, the people lost...

There is no difference between myself and them. Are we not all born on the same planet, only to ultimately return to the eternal heavens together in death?

O divine creator, answer me.

"Allow me to begin."

I address the attendants sitting around the table. The agency's conference room doubles as a drawing room. There are a total of seven workers present—office workers and detectives—and it wouldn't be an exaggeration to say these are most of our top members. It's extremely rare for them to gather like this. I pass out the necessary documents, then explain.

"I would like you all to refer to these documents concerning our situation. To summarize, our agency is currently being threatened. Someone has crafted a careful, devious scandal against us."

"Yeah, the agency's in trouble. We get it. Now get to the point and tell us about the bomb."

One of the attendees speaks up. It's the agency's personal physician, Dr. Yosano.

"Very well. This is an e-mail I received from the offender. It will help profile the criminal as well, so please make sure to read it."

Dear Sir,

I hope everyone at the Armed Detective Agency is doing well. I would first like to extend my deepest gratitude to you all for your support in investigating the abandoned building. Now, I know this is quite sudden, but I am contacting you in hopes of asking you another favor.

Only a few moments ago, we set a massive bomb somewhere in town. Therefore, for the safety of the people, I would like for you to promptly find this explosive and dispose of it. Furthermore, this bomb is set to detonate tomorrow at sundown, so I strongly urge that you solve this case before then.

This explosive we created is the same type of bomb that robbed the world of over one hundred precious lives during a certain incident in the past. What a horrendous event that was. The everlasting flames and blinding corona made it seem as if the sun itself had fallen out of the sky. The buildings fell one after another while innocent people's skin melted as they struggled to escape. The ground liquefied, and vehicles were knocked into the buildings like spears. I could describe it only as hell on earth. That is why I beg that your agency makes their best effort to prevent something like that from ever happening in Yokohama.

While I understand that this goes without saying, we shall be recording your agency's efforts just like last time. Please note that if you unfortunately fail to disarm the bomb, we will once again release the footage to the public.

With best wishes to you, I pray for your health and success.

Yours sincerely,
The Azure Apostle

"...What kind of sick person writes a thing like that?" Dr. Yosano scoffs.

"I completely agree. It is more than evident that this so-called Azure Apostle is the one who recorded the incident at the abandoned hospital and released it to the public to tarnish our agency's name. And now it appears they are threatening us again."

"So you believe the offender's objective is to hurt our agency's reputation?" the president calmly inquires.

"Most likely."

The Armed Detective Agency has fought through hell on multiple occasions. You would need an army to take us down in a battle of brute force. However, as long as we are a commercial corporation in the service industry built on the trust of our clients, a scandal like this would make us vulnerable. If the news spreads that we failed to disarm the bomb, and if there is any judicial intervention, then the agency's reputation will be ruined. We would be driven out of business.

"Do you have any idea as to where the bomb is?"

"The terrorist insinuated that it's somewhere that could kill and injure over a hundred people, so we have workers currently searching for possible locations. However, there are countless candidates, such as stations and skyscrapers, so finding the bomb before time runs out could be next to impossible."

"How about we start off by searching for surveillance video cables?"

As mentioned in the e-mail, the Azure Apostle would have to record us failing and leak those videos to the public in order to tarnish our reputation. Therefore, they would most likely be using equipment to secretly videotape us just like last time, but...

"If the surveillance equipment or wiretaps used the latest batteries, they would be able to record a few days' worth of footage. They could also be small and shaped like a die or fountain pen, even, and able to wirelessly transmit data up until the explosion destroys them. Realistically speaking, finding the surveillance equipment would prove to be an even more difficult task than finding the bomb. Just in case, I have been asking distributors if they know of anyone purchasing a large number of said devices, but the answers I've received so far have been less than ideal."

"Any records of criminals who go by the name Azure Apostle?"

"We haven't found any such records so far."

Azure Apostle. The only difference from the first e-mail is the fact that the client signed off with their name. There has to be a reason for that. All we can say for sure right now is that the Azure Apostle is knowledgeable about explosives and is, for whatever reason, trying to run the agency into the ground.

"I'm currently in contact with an affiliate who's making a list of candidates who specialize in explosives and may have a grudge against the agency."

"Still unable to get in contact with Ranpo?" Dr. Yosano asks.

I'm fairly sure the president himself has been keeping in touch with Ranpo...

"I spoke with him this morning," the president replies, crossing his arms. "He said the incident in Kyushu is about to reach a conclusion, so he should be on his way back soon. However, it's unlikely he will be able to return before sundown."

Ranpo Edogawa is a skill user and the top detective we have at this agency. Assault, kidnapping, murder—no matter the crime, his extraordinary skill, *Super Deduction*, allows him to reveal the truth. We would have been able to solve this case in no time if he was here...but unfortunately, he is in Kyushu handling another case at the request of a central government

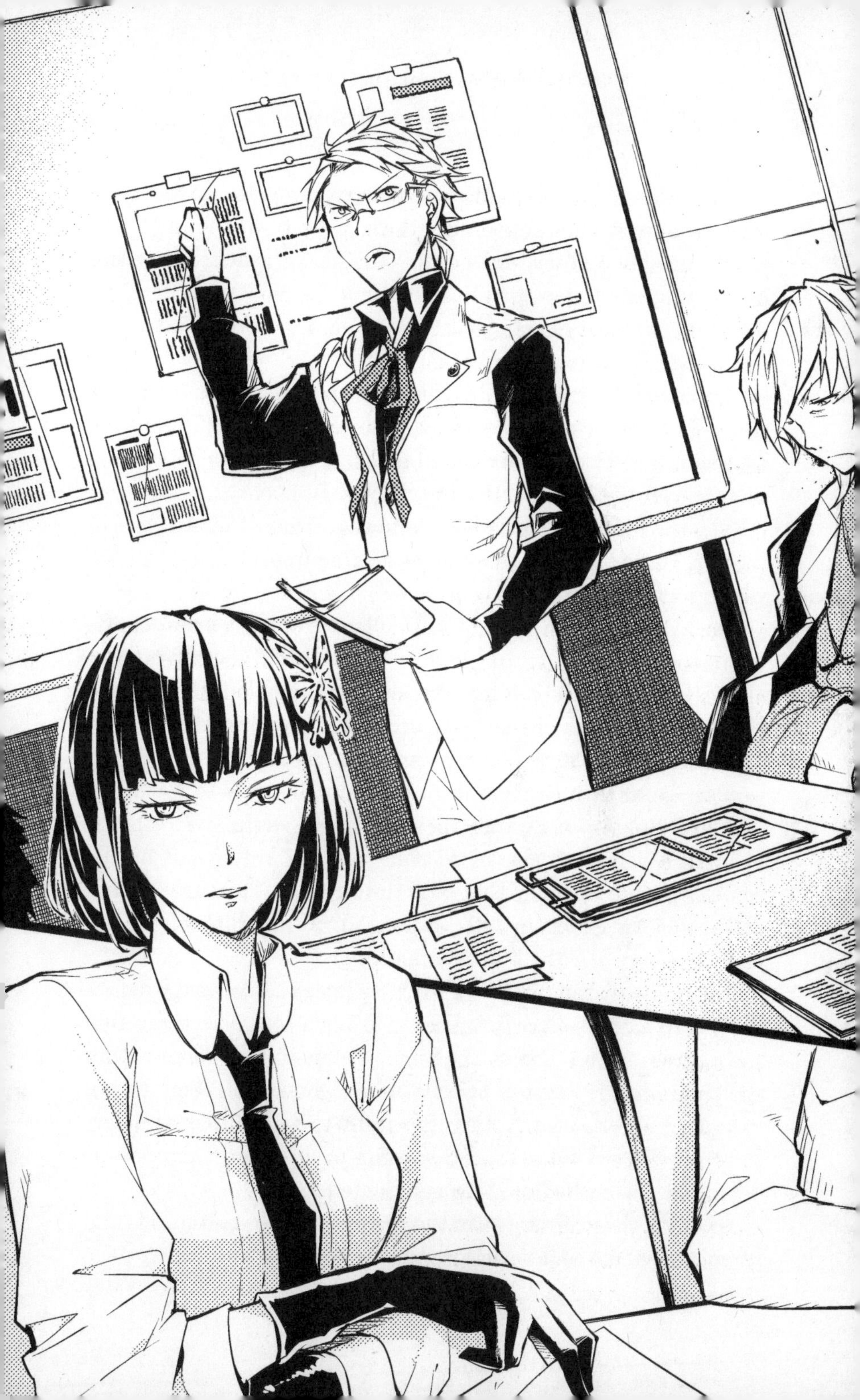

official. Ranpo's investigating a bizarre murder case where a white-haired man supposedly came back from the dead and killed his wife and best friend, so he is not in a situation where he can immediately return to Yokohama.

"Would it be possible to have an interview with this taxi driver in custody?" the president asks.

"The driver is currently on board a special military aircraft that is still in the sky as we speak. It's keeping him safe from any assassination attempts by the Mafia, but it also makes getting an interview with him extremely difficult."

Even the Mafia wouldn't be able to reach their target if he's in the sky. Unfortunately, that makes getting information from our witness a difficult task as well.

"I will speak with the military police's intelligence department. I want you to get in contact with whoever you can on that aircraft and have the cabdriver answer our questions in writing."

"I'll prepare the necessary documents immediately."

It's unlikely that the cabdriver is the Azure Apostle. It just wouldn't make sense for him to go out of his way to e-mail us with information on where the kidnapped victims were being held. In a way, he's also a "victim" who got ratted out by the Azure Apostle. But then that begs the question: How are the taxi driver and the Azure Apostle connected? At any rate, all we can do now is hope that he knows something.

"Everyone, listen up. What we have here is a cowardly attack on the Armed Detective Agency. We have two objectives: find the aggressor and disarm the bomb. Defusing the bomb within the time limit is our top priority. If we allow that bomb to kill anyone, then we do not have the right to call ourselves detectives anymore. Understand that your pride as humans, not as detectives, is on the line. Now get started."

And with those orders from the president, everyone stands and promptly begins to take action.

◇ ◇ ◇

The investigation is so busy that there is hardly a moment to breathe. The deadline is sundown today. Until then, we have to search the city and find that bomb. There's no time.

I think back to the investigation that led to this and pick up the phone. I asked Rokuzo to trace the first e-mail, which could potentially help solve this case. After listening to the phone ring for a while, Rokuzo finally picks up.

"Heeey... This is Taguchi. Sorry I'm not...yaaawn...here right now. Seeya."

"I don't have time for your games. This is urgent."

"Oh, is that you, Four-Eyes? Do you have any idea what time it is? It's nine in the morning, for cryin' out loud!"

"You're the only one still sleeping at nine in the morning, you social misfit. Start acting like a normal person and go outside more. It's good for your health."

"Tsk. Who d'you think you are, my dad?"

"No, I—"

I can't be your father. I swallow the words before they slip off my tongue.

"Anyway, there's been a change of plans. I need you to trace that client's e-mail and find out who they are as quickly as possible. Have you made any progress?"

"Oh, that? It turned out to be a lot more difficult than I thought. I won't get technical on you, but they're using multiple hubs to hide their tracks. This wasn't the work of an amateur."

I am already painfully aware of that.

"I received another e-mail from the same sender. Could you find the source if you had that?"

"It would help, but I can't say anything for sure until I try... There are other ways to do this, though."

"What do you mean?"

"I could send a virus to the hub and use it to trace the source from there. It'd take some work, but it's reliable. I'd kind of have to break the law, though."

"It's fine. The ends justify the means. Do it."

"Whoa. You serious? You, Mr. By-the-Book? I'm recording this call, y'know. What if I told you to hand over the recording of me hacking into your detective agency in exchange for this conversation?"

"Then I'd do it. Just hurry, okay?"

I never planned on handing it over to the authorities in the first place. I just said that to have an excuse to get Rokuzo's assistance. Apparently, he hasn't figured that out, though.

"Wow. How generous of you, Four-Eyes. You better have some cash waiting for me when this is over."

The phone clicks. I ponder in silence with the receiver still in hand. This is no time to get sentimental. The bomb is top priority. We're going to have the deaths of innocent lives on our hands if we don't find it in time. Still, we have no leads. Damn it. What the hell is Dazai thinking, disappearing at a time like this?

⬡ ⬡ ⬡

It isn't long before I find Dazai during my search downtown. He's at an old-fashioned café facing the road, trying to chat up a woman.

"Is this your first time in Yokohama? I could show you around if you want."

"Really? You would do that for me? But I'd feel terrible... I mean, it sounds as if things are rather chaotic at the detective agency with the bomb threat. You even said Detective Kunikida has been busy with phone calls and the investigation all morning."

"He's a workaholic—a real glutton for punctuality. I mean, get this: If you tell him to meet you at around twelve o'clock, he'll show within ten seconds of twelve every time. What is he, a train?"

"Oh my... You don't say."

"Dazai! What do you think you're doing, skipping work?! And don't use me in your attempts to pick up women!"

"Oh, and when we were at this abandoned hospital, Kunikida thought he saw a ghost, and he started shrieking like a little girl—"

"Don't ignore me!"

I slap Dazai on the back of the head while he merrily chats with Miss Sasaki.

"Ouch! What was that for, Kunikida? Hmm? ...Kunikida? How long have you been there?"

"Don't play dumb. You knew I was behind you. Anyway, what do you think you're doing? We have a dire emergency on our hands, and you're out on some kind of fancy date? Not only that, you're out with a victim from one of our cases!"

"Are you jealous?"

"I'm not jealous!"

I am in no way jealous. Absolutely not.

"Come on—don't be like that. She was almost killed by some monster. The poor gal's traumatized. Isn't it our duty as a detective agency to protect her and provide emotional support? And from my experience, it takes only a smile and some kindness to get a woman swooning over you when she's fallen on hard times."

"You should have just shut up while you were ahead."

...*I'll have to write that tidbit down in my notebook later.*

"Besides, how could someone as flippant as you even have a chance?"

Surely a woman this beautiful must already be seeing someone.

"And that's just what makes you Doppo Kunikida. I asked, and she doesn't have a family or anyone she can go to. Also, she and her boyfriend separated not too long ago."

...I remember her mentioning she didn't have anyone to turn to, but I had no idea it was this severe.

"So she's available, Kunikida." Dazai grins, gently elbowing me in the side.

"Available for what?"

I'll just make a face like I have no idea what he's talking about.

"Listen, Dazai. I came here to fill you in on what we discussed at this morning's meeting, which you so happened to skip. And if I catch you skipping again, I'm going to take every appropriate measure to successfully resuscitate you the next time you try to kill yourself."

"Oh, that's dirty. You're sick, Kunikida."

Dazai makes a disgusted expression. Satisfied, I place the documents in hand on the table and spread them out.

"This is the latest information. We received a recording of the kidnapper's statement during the military police's questioning. It appears he admitted to kidnapping the victims and gassing them so they couldn't escape. However, that's all he admitted. He claims he didn't know about the surveillance equipment, and it's unlikely he would lie about it now. That's why—"

"There must be *at least two people* behind this, right? The person who kidnapped the victims and the person who recorded everything: The former is the driver, while the latter is the Azure Apostle, I'm guessing?"

"Conceivably, yes."

"Um..." Miss Sasaki timidly speaks up. "Are you sure I should be listening to this? Wouldn't this fall under confidential information?"

"You're a victim, Miss Sasaki, and you're just as much a part of this as we are, so don't worry about a thing. If you weren't, Mr. Stickler-for-Rules right here wouldn't have started explaining things with you around."

"I am not particularly strict about rules. This is normal."

"See? He even jokes around sometimes. Hilarious, am I right? Anyway, any new leads on the criminal we're after?"

"I'm completely normal."

"...Sorry, you're right. It's completely normal. So can you continue filling me in on what's going on?"

Why did he apologize?

"We looked into the cabdriver's history, and as far as we could tell, he had no connections with any underground shady businesses. The data makes him seem like nothing more than your ordinary taxi driver. He has no criminal history and no reputation for hanging with the wrong crowd. And yet, I have a hard time believing he came up with the idea to kidnap people and sell their insides to an organ-trafficking syndicate on his own. Someone must have told him about this get-rich-quick scheme."

"Someone like the Azure Apostle? Couldn't we just ask the driver who told him?"

"He won't tell us. He thinks if he talks, they'll really kill him this time. I'd love to pull each and every hair off his head until he gives us something, but unfortunately, he's under heavy surveillance over the clouds right now. We'd run out of time before we could pull enough strings to get an interview with him."

Just who's behind all this? Not only did they approach the taxi driver with the organ trade offer, set up surveillance equipment in that abandoned hospital, and make a bomb, they also set said bomb somewhere in the city and are trying to threaten the agency. But why? What are they after?

"I hope I'm not overstepping my boundaries here, but..." Miss Sasaki suddenly speaks up. "Do you think this Azure Apostle could be the criminal behind the Azure Banner Terrorist incident?"

"Hmm..."

The Azure Banner Terrorist case—the incident that cost Rokuzo's father his life. The moment I saw the word *azure* in his name, I briefly played with the idea myself.

"But the terrorist behind that incident, the Azure King, died in the blast as well. The dead cannot threaten the living. That much is certain in this world."

"Oh, so does that mean you're not afraid of ghosts anymore, Kunikida?"

"Never speak of ghosts again."

"But it was a large explosion, yes? I heard they never found the Azure King's body, either. What if he faked his death to escape and is now in hiding somewhere?"

I had wondered that myself, which is why I contacted the military police. However, they said that wasn't possible.

"According to police analyses, the Azure King undoubtedly perished in the blast. They have the latest forensic technology available, and some of their comrades died in the explosion as well, so it's hard to imagine they would overlook anything."

"But…"

"Well, I dunno much about this Azure King, but is he really someone who would crawl out of the pits of hell to take vengeance on the agency?"

Dazai's ignorance never ceases to amaze me.

I reluctantly explain. The Azure King was the mastermind behind the Azure Banner Terrorist incident that targeted and destroyed government facilities. He was known as the worst and most destructive domestic terrorist threat of postwar Japan.

Once said to be an excellent state government official before raising the azure banner, the ambitious youth graduated at the top of his class from an elite educational institution, then worked as a central civil servant in the executive and legislative world after studying abroad. Yet, somewhere along the line, he mysteriously began to aspire to cleanse society through its destruction.

Then one day, a certain video recording was sent to a major domestic broadcasting station. It was a video of a young man whose face had been obscured by an azure banner. He called himself the Azure King and claimed he was going to commit an act of terror. He then told of how he lamented for this imperfect world and that such imperfections could only be buried by other imperfections.

"No matter how much we aspire to, our neighbors will fall ill, our parents will die, and only a small fraction of evildoers will see justice. Then let us realize an ideal world, not by the hand of a god but by our own imperfect bloodstained hands."

And with those final words, three domestic government facilities were simultaneously attacked: The city police's associated facility was set on fire, something collided with a government vehicle, and a military post was hit with a bomb.

A later investigation revealed that the eight people he killed included a murderer who was found not guilty due to the prosecutor's insufficient paperwork, a member of parliament who was rumored to have been embezzling funds meant to aid refugees from industrializing nations, and a military platoon that beat a young military policeman to death before systematically covering up the act. These eight people all perished in the attack. The Azure King committed an act of evil to execute criminals who couldn't be punished by the law.

This blitz tactic shocked everyone. He was able to simultaneously attack and destroy multiple strictly guarded and heavily protected government facilities. Nobody even imagined such an attack was possible.

And the Azure King's terrorist acts continued further. Disgraced, the military and government gave nationwide orders to locate and arrest him. Even the detective agency was asked to help. What happened after that was exactly how I explained before. His hideout was discovered, and those who went inside were killed in his suicidal blast. The case was solved at the cost of innocent lives.

"But if the one behind this really is the Azure King, then why would he be so persistent in trying to tarnish the agency's name?"

"Maybe because you're the one he has a grudge against, Kunikida."

A grudge? Against me? I mean, I was the one who contacted the police and led them to his whereabouts, but... It can't be. The ghost of the Azure King, the worst terrorist this country has ever seen, returned from the grave to have his revenge on the agency and me because of a grudge?

"At any rate, we'd best keep our guard up until we know who we're dealing with. There's no way of knowing who's going to attack us or when they're going to do it. We have to take Miss Sasaki somewhere safe as well."

"Perhaps the agency office? Oh, but nobody's there at night. Hmm..."

That's when I suddenly catch on to what Dazai's up to.

"I seriously hope you're not trying to find an excuse to keep her at your place to 'protect' her, because I will not allow such lewd, immoral, unhealthy relations to continue any longer. Honestly, were you raised by savages or something? Absolutely appalling. If it were me, y'know, I'd first make her feel comfo—"

"Hold on, Kunikida. You know there's nothing going on between Miss Sasaki and me, right?"

"What?"

"Listen, the first day she stayed over, I slept in another room. I haven't laid a finger on her. C'mon, do you really think I'd try to seduce a woman who was almost killed earlier that day? I've got a little more sense than that. Besides, I'd have to deal with you if that ever happened, and I'd rather not."

Oh... It looks like I jumped to conclusions.

"I can't deny that I knew you had the wrong idea, and I just decided not to say anything 'cause it was funny, though."

You little...

That said, a pure, honest man such as myself could have had it much worse in this kind of situation. Dazai could have said something like "You assumed the worst all because she spent the night at my place? Gee, Kunikida, you're a real perv." I wouldn't be able to refute that, and I'd probably die an agonizing death on the spot. I guess I should just be thankful that didn't happen.

...But how could I not imagine something like that? This is Dazai we're talking about. In any case, if there is anything to be thankful for, it's that he's not some lecher who jumps on any woman he can get his hands on. Keeping a professional distance from the victim is more difficult than I thought.

"Just stop wasting my time, Dazai. If nothing happened, then we have nothing to worry about. But from now on, let's make sure to keep a healthy distance during work and forge proper relationships with our clients. This is what it means to be a professional."

"...I hear you." He firmly nods before facing Miss Sasaki once more. "So what's your type?"

"Didn't you just say you heard me?!"

I take it back. He *is* a lecher who would jump on any woman given the chance.

"M-my type...? I'm sorry; I just feel it would be rather presumptuous of me to seek out a specific type of man, but...I do find men who are passionate about their ideals and really devote themselves to something to be...very attractive."

...*Come again?*

"Aw man. You basically just described Kunikida! Looks like I never had a chance. Tsk. Well, you two enjoy the rest of your date. I'm gonna go make sure I still have all my fingers."

"D-Dazai, get back here!"

"What? Ugh, now I forgot what finger I was on!"

"Quit sulking and take a seat!"

You can't leave me alone with her! I wouldn't know what to talk about!

"But I'm just an ordinary woman. Even if I was with someone who lived for his ideals, I wouldn't be of any help. Even if I devoted myself to supporting those ideals, I would only end up getting in the way and exhausting us both... Ultimately, he would choose his ideals over me, and things would end there. So I think I will abstain from dating any idealists in the future."

There is a hint of sorrow in her smile...but why?

"You're so easy to read, Kunikida. You know that?"

"I—I wasn't thinking about anything in particular! Quit looking at me, Dazai!"

"Ouch!"

I twist Dazai's head until he's facing the opposite direction.

"First, you want me to sit. Now you want me to look the other way. Can you make up your mind? Anyway, can we just get back on topic?"

...What *were* we talking about again?

"Oh, about keeping Miss Sasaki somewhere safe, yes? Well, I do have some acquaintances with the police I could contact..."

"Hey, um...I really appreciate what you're trying to do for me, but I don't want to bother you any more than I already have... So please don't worry about me. I'll find a hotel to stay in tonight."

"I can't allow that. Hotels aren't safe, and sending you to one after the recent events would be in bad taste. Having said that, I wouldn't trust Dazai to keep his hands to himself if you stayed at his place again. Come stay at mine."

"Huh?"

"Huh?"

"D-don't get the wrong idea! I have no ulterior motives, if that's what you're implying!"

"Actually, from the way this conversation's been going, it sounds like an ulterior motive is all you have. You just don't know when to quit, eh?"

"It's not like that! I'm just genuinely—"

"Ah-ha-ha-ha! I'm kidding! Miss Sasaki, you'll be safe at

Kunikida's place. He doesn't have the courage to— *Ahem...* He is a man of ideals and virtue. Would you like to see his notebook? You should read the page about his ideal woman. It's *amazing*."

Dazai hands Miss Sasaki a notebook. Taken aback, I pat my pockets, but it's nowhere to be found.

"Dazai! When did you steal that from me?!"

"Here, it's this page."

He opens my notebook and points.

"Oh my... Are you sure this is okay?"

"You're curious, right?"

"Well...in all honesty...yes, I suppose I am slightly curious."

Miss Sasaki reads the notebook with a bashful smile before slowly turning pale.

"Huh? What does that...? Oh, I see. But this is..."

My ideal woman: a voluminous work consisting of eight pages, fifteen topics, and fifty-eight items.

"Huh?! ...Oh, so that means... Hmm... Ohhh..."

I remember what Dazai said: "*Never show this to a woman. It'd really turn them off.*" When Miss Sasaki lifts her head after reading, her expression is void of any and all joy. The only thing on her face is a chilling, lifeless smile, not unlike a statue's.

"Detective Kunikida."

"Yes...?"

"People like this don't exist."

◇ ◇ ◇

Someone bring me a stiff drink.

◇ ◇ ◇

It's located in the nation's capital, Tokyo, the heart of this country where the political and economic central functions intersect.

Foreigners of all races and creeds go in and out of this building—the *United States Embassy*, the largest foreign territory in Japan. Despite it being the afternoon, the people in the waiting room for general visitors are quietly whiling away the minutes and hours until their turn. They keep silent as if anticipating a judge's decision, staring off into space as if looking at something only they can see.

A live Major League Baseball game plays on the flat-screen TV installed on the wall, while a middle-aged Caucasian male wearing a black cap lazily criticizes his favorite team for allowing the other to score a run.

I look at Dazai at my side. He's smiling gleefully. He must be really looking forward to the mission. This is no laughing matter, though.

"Everything ready to go, Kunikida?"

"My stomach already hurts thinking about it. Please don't mess this up. We could be tried under international law if we aren't careful."

"International outlaws... Has a nice ring to it, doesn't it? All right, well, here goes nothing!"

"Hey...!"

Stricken with panic, I try to stop him, but he's already heading over to the information desk. Dazai is wearing a raggedy, patched-up undershirt while I'm dressed in a high-end navy business suit and tie. He stands in front of the embassy worker's desk and obnoxiously opens his big mouth.

"Hey, you! How much longer do I hafta wait?! I've been here for *siiix whooole hooours!*"

Everybody in the vicinity turns around and stares. The Japanese lady working reception blinks in astonishment.

"I don't wanna wait anymore! I can't...! I just can't take it! Lemme talk to your boss right now!"

Dazai thrashes his arms and legs about as he continues to

mouth off to the receptionist. Though this may be part of the mission, it's painful to watch another adult act this way. I would rather drink poison and die than do *that*.

"Excuse me... What was it you needed again?" she asks, puzzled. Her handling of the situation is admirable, but she's outclassed.

"I toldja, didn't I?! I wanna seek refuge! R-E-F-U-G-E! I'm here for refuge in your honorable nation! But you're making me wait foreeever! Does that mean you're refusing my request? Is that it? Missy, you've got a lot of nerve making political decisions like this! You've got no right!"

"You there! What do you think you're doing?! Causing a distur- bance in the embassy is a serious offense, you know!"

Naturally, the guards at the entrance start rushing toward Dazai. Looks like I'm up.

"Stop right there. That man making a fuss over there is with me. Do you have the authority to arrest him?" I stand before the rushing guards. "Vienna Convention on Consular Relations, article thirty-one, paragraph two! 'The authorities of the receiv- ing State shall not enter that part of the consular premises that is used exclusively for the purpose of the work of the consular post except with the consent of the head of the consular post or of his designee or of the head of the diplomatic mission of the sending State.' That man is a guest of the embassy until deemed a hindrance by the consular post. Stopping him without permis- sion could turn this into an international issue!"

My loud rebuke puzzles the guards.

They obviously know the Vienna Convention on Consular Relations by heart, but it's only natural to flinch when someone screams "international issue" at you.

"Hey, Boss! I need *refuuuge*! BOSSSSSS!!"

Dazai throws a temper tantrum on the floor in front of the information desk. While it's a relief knowing the guards can't stop him, there's a part of me that wants to forget the mission and kill him.

Now, there's a reason why the Armed Detective Agency is using a five-year-old's tactics to attack the embassy, an important, high-toned diplomatic establishment.

"The bomber is from another country?" I ask. We're back at that same street-side café.

"Yeah, and a pro, at that," Dazai replies while sipping his coffee. He first pointed this out to me after Miss Sasaki got off the phone with a colleague from her university.

"My college major was criminal psychology. Perhaps I know something that could be of use," she'd said.

I hear Miss Sasaki is well-known in her community as a criminal psychology researcher. It seems she's a talented young associate professor whose work has been recognized by several famous academic conferences, which is why she's been independently scrutinizing similar past crimes detailed in a fellow researcher's work.

"I contacted a colleague in my field regarding similar cases, but their investigation concluded that there has not been a single bombing incident in Japan that has claimed over a hundred lives as mentioned in the e-mail... Of course, this is excluding those who died in the war."

"Have there been incidents like this abroad, then?"

"Yes... There have been a few dozen terrorist attacks in other countries, revolving around ideology and political conflict. However, there is little data for these cases that would provide details such as the type of bomb used or the manufacturer... I'm sorry I couldn't be of any help."

"No, that's really good information. This would mean the Azure Apostle knew the composition and structure of the explosive used in those bombings when they made the one to set in Yokohama. I feel like we're now one step closer to finding our guy, don't you think?"

"That said, we still haven't figured out where they hid the bomb. Do you really think we'll be able to find it in time at this rate?"

At the very least, we need to find out this person's name and what they look like. There's no other way to locate the bomb.

Dazai places a thumb on his chin as if deep in thought.

"The bomber is in hiding... There's no way we're going to find them," he suddenly mutters. "...Guess I have to do it myself."

"Do what?"

"Kunikida, in the e-mail, they said they'd 'made' the bomb, right? But can you really make a bomb that could kill hundreds that easily?"

"It wouldn't be easy for the average person, but someone with extensive knowledge probably wouldn't have much difficulty."

Even I have a certain amount of knowledge of hazardous chemicals, since I'm currently pursuing a degree in science and mathematics. Besides, I also work on dangerous jobs at the agency. Chemical production for explosives requires utmost caution, especially in regard to temperature and impact. Even the smallest mistake could cause an unwanted catastrophe. The ingredients themselves, however, are simple and could even be found in an elementary school's science room. Hydrochloric acid, nitric acid, nitrogen fertilizer, aluminum: All of these can be legally purchased for cheap. The combination ratio, order of procedure, transportation, and technique for detonating the bomb are where things get tricky.

"Some say that each pro has their own recipe, which acts as their brand when they sell their explosives, but..."

"Exactly. That's why I don't think it'd be easy to replicate a bomb that was used in some previous terrorist attack."

"So what you're saying is...the person who made this bomb is the same person who made the bomb in that incident that killed over a hundred people?"

"Not only that, the way it was described in the e-mail was oddly visually specific, don't you think?"

I check the e-mail again. *"The everlasting flames and blinding corona made it seem as if the sun itself had fallen out of the sky. The buildings fell one after another while innocent people's skin melted as they struggled to escape. The ground liquefied, and vehicles were knocked into the buildings like spears."*

"This is just speculation on my part, but doesn't it sound a bit like he's describing what he saw?"

"What?"

"Miss Sasaki, is there any news footage showing any of the past bombings abroad?"

"No, I'm afraid not. Filming an explosion that large was probably the last thing on the victims' minds as well."

"Normally, I'd agree with you, but the e-mail vividly details what just happened minutes after the explosion. Maybe they set the bomb, ran away, and came back after the explosion in time to see all this?"

"In other words, the bomber who killed all those people in the past is the Azure Apostle?"

If that's the case, then that would narrow down who the criminal might be. We're looking at a bomb expert who was abroad during that incident and is currently in Japan. But...

"We still don't have enough information to go by."

"Why?"

"I suppose I will fill you in, since you decided to skip the meeting. The Public Security Intelligence Agency and military police–affiliated organizations already looked into domestic bomb-making experts, and they didn't find any suspects. Nobody on the list of Japanese candidates possesses the refined technology needed for high-grade explosives that could kill or injure over one hundred people, nor are there any bomb manufacturer candidates they don't already have their eye on. Having said that, it's not like we could go around questioning every non-Japanese person we see."

"Heh-heh." Dazai smirks.

"What are you so obnoxiously giddy about?"

"While even the military police come to the famous detective agency for help from time to time, there's still one directory nobody wants us to see: information held by foreign intelligence agencies. I'm sure they have records on past bombing suspects."

"A foreign intelligence agency...?"

The most famous intelligence agencies that come to mind are the CIA and NSA in the United States and MI6 in the United Kingdom. They conduct covert operations all around the world for their home countries' safety and prosperity. However...

"Foreign intelligence agencies aren't just going to hand over confidential information to private Japanese enterprises. Do you even know anybody working for an intelligence agency in the first place?"

"Nope."

"I figured."

"But I know where to meet one."

—*I've got a bad feeling about this.*

And that's how our undercover mission at the embassy began. The plan Dazai came up with is simple: One of us makes a scene at the embassy, and if we're lucky, one of the higher-ups will come over to bring things under control. Then we can talk with that high government official to negotiate. For a secret agent abroad, their home country's embassy is not only a base but a place of peace and comfort as well. The embassy must have some sort of connection with their country's secret agents.

While it's a reckless, aggressive plan, Dazai's idea sheds a glimmer of hope on a seemingly desperate mission. During our work together, I at times find his wits and critical-thinking skills nothing short of amazing. There is no telling what he's capable of. I can't help but feel that hidden behind his eccentric behavior lurks something chilling—a devilish wisdom of some kind.

I have a difficult time believing he's just some wanderer with no real background. Whenever I try to ask him about his past, he avoids the question. While I refuse to press him for answers, I wonder if he has a dark past. *Could he have been in an illegal—?*

"Awww, c'mon, lady! Just grant my asylum already! Pretty pleeease? C'mon, don't look away from me when I'm talkin' to you! Look at me! Yeah, like that! Keep lookin' at me like that!"

—No. He's just an idiot.

"Um… Could you please write your name on the waiting list?" The receptionist timidly pulls out a sheet of paper.

"I've already filled out one of those!" Dazai yells. He's lying, of course. "I even made sure to complete all the parts in fine print with my favorite fountain pen, and I'm still not gettin' any service. Why d'you think I came here to talk to you, huh?"

He whips out a thick coal-black fountain pen from his breast pocket to show her.

"This fountain pen is the same kind that was used by a Middle Eastern dictator. Pretty cool, huh? You can have a look if you want. Here. It's long and heavy, so it's extremely hard to write with. I had to use this to fill out all those little spaces over and over again. You can see why I'm mad now, right?"

It's your fault for using that pen in the first place!

I keep that thought to myself, though.

"Listen, lady, I'm an author, mmkay? Ever read any of my books? Here, I'll even make you the protagonist in my next story, so please just lemme speak to one of your higher-ups. I'll write a book about us committing lovers' suicide. I'll even use this pen to write it if you help me defect."

For a terrible author, he's becoming curiously good at this acting thing. I get the sense this is how he woos women at pubs.

"C'mon, throw me a bone here. I'm in a lot of trouble. Big trouble! Some scary guys from the PSIA are coming for my neck! Listen, I just write whatever I like, and all I said was that one of the Foreign Affairs ministers was wearing a toupee, and now the authorities are trying to kill me! This is a violation of free speech, and I will not allow the government to abuse their authority! And down with hairpieces!"

"Shut the hell up, will ya?! I'm tryin' to watch the game here! And what's your problem with toupees?!" the Caucasian man in the black cap watching the baseball game shouts hoarsely, but it's going to take more than that to bring Dazai down.

"Hey, I'm not the problem here! It's the guy who got mad at me for calling him out! If he was gonna get that upset about it, then he shoulda just shown us all his shiny bald pate and been proud of it!"

"E-excuse me, sir? You're, um, you're with him, c-correct?" the flustered office worker asks me with pleading eyes. *Apologies, but this is all for the greater good.*

"I'm his chief editor. While I sympathize with you, as you can see, he's in no mood to listen. If a civil servant with authority, however, was to come and talk with him directly, I guarantee he'd give up. So do you think you could talk to one of your superiors for me?"

"Okay..."

Drained of energy and in a state of shock, the receptionist nods before staggering to her feet.

"I'll be right back...with someone to help you..."

She probably feels that she's done everything she could and just doesn't want to deal with Dazai anymore. I don't blame her. I truly pity the woman.

After waiting for a short while, she returns and waves Dazai and me into another room.

"This way, please."

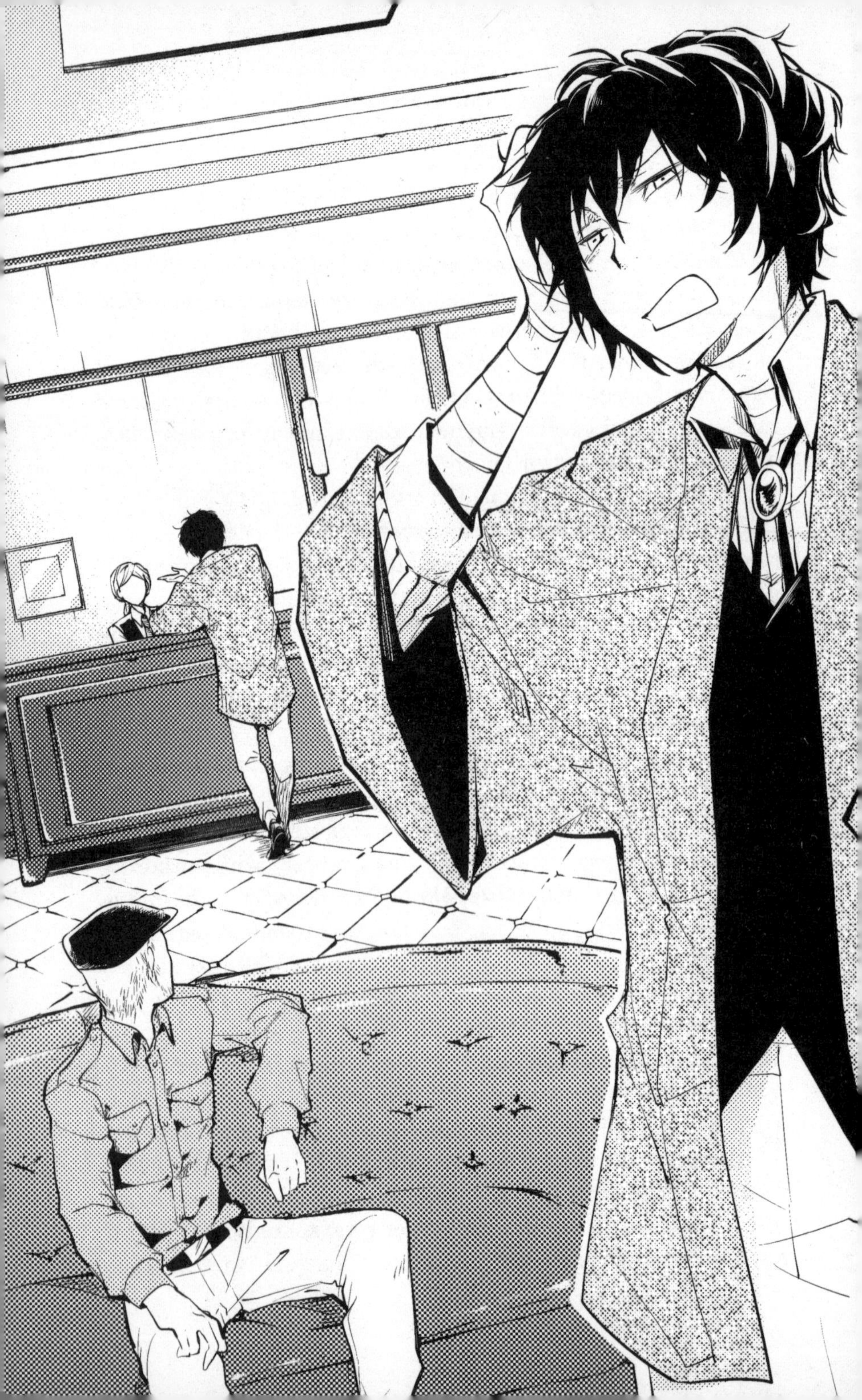

*   *   *

"You're making things really difficult for me, you know?"

We're taken to a diplomatic reception room where a bald Caucasian diplomat appears to have been waiting for us. The business card handed to us says he's a third attaché. Not a bad catch. But it's not enough. He isn't ranked high enough to know intelligence-agency secrets, which means only one thing: This is where the real mission starts.

"I completely understand, sir."

I lower my head. To someone from a different culture, bowing might confuse them, but it's surely not going to make them feel better.

"Never in my career have I ever heard of someone seeking political asylum from a country as peaceful as this one. I could contact our State Department, but I know the answer is going to be no. Therefore—"

"Oh, I don't care about that anymore. Sorry for the trouble. I mean, I really appreciate you taking the time to speak with us, but to tell the truth, I'm not actually an author."

I take out a black notebook with gold-framed letters.

"We're with the *Tokyo Metropolitan Police Department's Public Security Bureau.*"

"S-security...police...?" the attaché asks in astonishment.

I don't blame him. The situation is a lot more serious when you believe you're talking to the recipient country's security police.

"Due to the circumstances, we needed to take an unconventional route in establishing contact. However, this notebook should serve as proof that we are who we say we are."

I hold up my police notebook with the words PUBLIC SECURITY BUREAU written in gold on the black cover. Inside sits my picture beside my division's name. The attaché opens my notebook and compares the picture to me. Of course, it's a fake I created with my skill, *The Matchless Poet*, but it appears every bit as real as an official one. Therefore, he has no way of knowing just by looking at it that we're lying.

—But what happens next determines whether we're in the clear.

"For certain reasons, we must secretly obtain information possessed by your country's intelligence agency. We would like for you to provide data on bomb engineering specialists within Japan. This is an issue of national security, so we need to be quick."

In one breath, I deliver the whole monologue I memorized prior to our arrival.

"Th-this is absurd."

"I know it's a lot to ask." I double down. "If you do not possess the information we need, then could you introduce us to someone who does?"

"There are indeed people from the intelligence agency who come here, but... This is not quite that simple."

"This is a time-sensitive matter. The lives of at least a hundred innocent people are on the line."

The attaché turns pale the moment he hears that people could die. He seems like a good person.

"P-please give me a moment."

Sweating profusely in fear, he picks up the telephone and calls someone. Speaking in almost a whisper, he argues with them for a while, then hangs up before facing us again.

"Oh, thank goodness," the attaché says with a smile. "We usually cannot accept such requests, but..."

I internally let out a sigh of relief, thrilled with how perfect things seem to be going. "Thank you very much."

"I spoke with the secretary on the phone, and she told me that my boss just happens to be having a meal with the Public Security Bureau's director right now. My boss probably won't be able to refuse a request from someone so high up. Phew. Thank goodness."

"...What?"

"Your boss should be here in around ten minutes. Please make yourselves at home until then."

He wipes the sweat off his forehead, a relieved smile on his face.

......This isn't good.

This is not good at all.

The Public Security Bureau's director has the same amount of authority as the chief of the Metropolitan Police, but he probably doesn't even have a clue about the bomb threat. Even if he did, he would never agree to go along with a scheme—let alone one by imposters—to steal confidential information from a foreign intelligence agency, especially when we still have no way to prove a bomb even exists.

"No, we... That wouldn't be good."

"Hmm? Oh, don't worry about a thing. The intelligence agency surely wouldn't ignore a request from someone as important as the Public Security Bureau's director. So please make yourselves at home. I insist."

What are we going to do? This entire mission will have been for nothing if the director shows up.

"That really wouldn't be good. Because... Uh..."

The attaché stares back at me in befuddlement.

"The director cannot come here...for various reasons."

"Are you sure? What reasons would that be?"

Damn it. I'm terrible at improvising.

"He's...very busy right now. He has a lot to do."

"I am sure he is quite busy, but they told me on the phone he could come and that it wouldn't be a problem."

"Yes, that's not what I meant, though. While he claims it wouldn't be a problem, he has...many errands."

"...?"

"Like...meeting an acquaintance who he'll end up chatting with for hours, going to the public office to turn in some documents, going to the store to pick up some dog food..."

"What is he, a housewife?" He tilts his head to the side, puzzled. Ugh. I don't even know what I'm talking about anymore.

"A-anyway, we cannot let the director know any of this."

"Do you mean...you came here without telling him?"

"No, we, uh— Well...yes. Yes we did."

"That's certainly no good. Why didn't you tell him?"

"We forgot."

"You forgot?!" He's completely dumbfounded.

"Yes, we... We were in a hurry, since it's an emergency, so we forgot to call him. So, you know, it was a state of emergency...so we forgot to call him."

"Was there a reason why you said it twice?"

"I have already told you all I'm permitted to say. Anyway, just bring us an intelligence operative to speak with!"

Because the more I talk, the deeper this hole gets!

"You do realize what you're asking from me, yes? The whereabouts of our intelligence operatives are secret. An explanation like the one you gave isn't—"

"Yeesh... Guess I've got no choice, then." Dazai heaves a sigh, then leans in. "First, I apologize for my inarticulate subordinate. Allow me to explain, sir. We had no choice but to come here in secret. There's a mole in the Public Security Bureau who's feeding information to the bomber, and we have reason to believe he's a close adviser to the director."

"What?"

"We're working with internal investigators to identify the criminal and the mole leaking intel, which is why we had to come undercover. We fear the mole may detonate the bomb if they figure out we're meeting with the director. So before that happens, we must find where this bomb is hidden."

The attaché's face turns pale. "Th-that certainly is a serious problem. You should have just said so," he says, glancing at me.

"The reason my colleague didn't say anything was because he

was afraid of a leak. He may be a terrible liar, but he does it to protect confidential information. If you were in our shoes, would you just casually tell the police that your boss might be a mole?"

"You have a point..." He nods in agreement.

"Fortunately, we are close to figuring out who our bomber is. He was the mastermind behind a large-scale terrorist bombing overseas sometime in the past. This is an important investigation for the national security of your country, one which also protects the world from terrorists. With the help of your intelligence agency, I want to clean the streets of these antiestablishment incendiaries hiding in the system. So could I ask for your cooperation?"

"Very well. I am at your service."

Dazai......... That was... That was amazing...

"Come with me, please."

The attaché hastily stands and motions us to follow.

He takes us to a private office in the embassy's basement and, his expression tense, asks us to wait here. Dazai and I are the only ones left in the room.

"I'd appreciate it if you'd stop picking on my attaché. He's a really good person. In fact, that's all he is."

A familiar middle-aged man eventually walks into the office.

"You're... You're the man who was watching baseball in the waiting room... *You're* the US intelligence operative?"

It's the same middle-aged Caucasian man in the black cap who had been idly watching the ball game on TV earlier.

"My ID says I'm the office janitor, though."

He grabs the name tag on his chest and shows us.

"So what are two busy detectives from the *Armed Detective Agency* doing here?"

Dazai and I exchange glances.

"You knew?"

"It's my job to gather information on issues occurring in this country, and when an organization of skill users starts making a fuss first thing in the morning, you can bet word has already reached halfway around the world. We've had our eye on you ever since you walked into the embassy."

It seems the omniscience of intelligence agencies isn't limited to movies and novels after all.

"We're looking for the person who set a bomb in the city. They're also responsible for a similar bombing overseas that claimed the lives of over a hundred people. Is there anyone like that in your records? The offender said, 'The everlasting flames and blinding corona made it seem as if the sun itself had fallen out of the sky,' and—"

"Oh... I figured it was him." The intelligence operative shakes his head.

"You know who's behind this?"

"'An everlasting fire and blinding white light' sounds just like Alamta and his aluminum powder–based explosives. Here's his file."

The intelligence operative pulls out a stack of papers from within the cabinet.

"A man of Japanese descent, Zadkiel Alamta was a bomb purveyor for a Middle Eastern terrorist organization. We've been keeping tabs on him ever since he entered the country a year ago."

"Without even telling the authorities in Japan?" I retort as I pore over the documents.

"We had our reasons. We wanted to capture him ourselves. Not only is he a bomber, he also sells explosives to terrorists of the same trade. If only we had his list of customers, we could arrest countless anti-American terrorists."

I flip through the pages where I see Alamta's photograph and the details of his past crimes.

"There honestly couldn't be a worse bomb composition."

I tightly clench my jaw.

"There are going to be a lot more than a hundred dead if this thing goes off in Yokohama."

Alamta specializes in railroad car bombs that contain a mixture of aluminum powder in slurry explosives. After placing a few hundred pounds of explosives in the passenger car, he lights the fuse remotely using a small electronic transmitter, such as a cell phone. He uses ammonium nitrate as his main raw material and acetone peroxide as an auxiliary material. Both ingredients are cheap, so bombs can be manufactured in high volumes.

Judging by the composition detailed in the documents, anyone within a radius of about 650 feet of the blast would die instantly, and people out of range would be showered in the liquefied aluminum and exposed to the extreme temperatures from the blast wave.

The only reason Alamta uses aluminum is to make sure he kills as many people as possible. Aluminum is a combustion promoter, which emits a blinding white light and increases the intensity of the explosive flames when it burns. Simultaneously, the blast waves would carry it, creating a cloud of extremely hot dust reaching over a thousand degrees Fahrenheit, which could burn the flesh right off a human body. To make matters worse, aluminum reacts with water to create a flammable hydrogen gas, meaning any contact with water would make more fire. Therefore, using the water from a fire hydrant to put out the blaze would only worsen it, making rescue operations difficult.

"The everlasting flames and blinding corona made it seem as if the sun itself had fallen out of the sky." He wasn't exaggerating. The bomb is as dreadful as it sounds. If a bomb goes off in a densely populated place in the city, casualties could exceed a thousand when considering secondary disasters such as blackouts and other fatal accidents. Moreover, a train bomb could easily sneak past the police and into the city. We absolutely cannot allow it to be detonated in Yokohama.

"Where is Alamta right now?"

"He threw my colleague off his trail and went into hiding two days ago. We figured he was getting ready to do something."

Damn it. It looks like we'll have to start searching for Alamta before we can find the bomb. I guess learning the bomber's name and background is a step forward, though. It is highly likely that Alamta and the Azure Apostle are one and the same. However, it's still unclear why he would threaten the detective agency. If he does have a grudge against us, then perhaps looking into the agency's past solved cases could lead to some clues.

"So, Mr. Spy, what do you want in return for this information?" Dazai chimes in with a chuckle.

"Nothing. I can't just sit back and watch hundreds of lives lost, even if they're another country's citizens. I am doing this for justice. I'll gladly provide you with any information you need."

"Yeah, right. I dunno about Kunikida here, but I'm just a bit more cynical than that," he replies with a grin. An American intelligence operative's job is to advance the prosperity and security of his country, after all. The agent ponders in silence for a while before responding.

"...If you catch Alamta, hand him over to us, not the Public Security Bureau. He's going to give us a list of his customers whether he likes it or not."

"Hand him over to you?" I knit my brow. "If he truly is behind all this, shouldn't you be questioning him along with the Japanese authorities?"

"About that, Kunikida. These guys plan on *torturing* the bomber for information, and with methods so brutal they're prohibited by international law. See, they wouldn't be able to use such unethical means if they were to cooperate with another nation's authorities. That's why they want to take him into custody without anyone knowing."

"......"

I look at the agent, who is silent and expressionless. It's evident he's not looking to make any excuses. Criminals aren't the only ones who break the law and violate ethical standards. Nevertheless, a foreign secret intelligence agency won't change their ways, regardless of how a nobody like myself might feel about it.

"This isn't an official meeting, and you haven't leaked any information. Therefore, there is no reason for us to provide anything in return. Come, Dazai; we're leaving."

After urging Dazai to get up, I turn on my heel and head for the door.

"Tell the receptionist you're from Fenimore Transport from now on. They'll let me know you're here. Anyway, I'm impressed you were able to make it this far with almost no clues. You have talent. If you're ever fired from the detective agency, get in touch with me. We could use an agent like you."

"Wow. What'll it be, Kunikida?"

"I have no interest in joining an organization that doesn't bat an eye even after hearing that a terrorist plans on bombing Japan. We'll be leaving now."

I depart the office without even waiting for a response. The agent remains silent.

○ ○ ○

Dazai and I return to the detective agency to organize the information from the documents. Approximately two hours remain until sundown. We have to capture the bomber Alamta and force him to tell us where the explosive is...within a mere two hours. We're not without good news, though. I received some reassuring information when I contacted the agency. The moment I heard the news, I became certain: We can disarm this bomb.

"Ah-ha-ha-ha! You guys would be lost without me!"

I hear his usual boisterous laughter the moment I return to the office.

"Ranpo! How did the case in Kyushu go?"

"Oh, that? I took one look at the body and figured out who did it and how."

The man mirthfully sipping on his drink as he talks is Ranpo Edogawa, a senior colleague.

"I heard what happened, Kunikida. Everyone's been running in circles over some little bomb, huh? I really wish my colleagues could take care of themselves sometimes. You know, I didn't even get the chance to sightsee in Kyushu thanks to you. Man, I really wanted to eat some *onsen tamago*, too."

"You have my apologies. However, we need your help."

"My help?"

"Yes. Unfortunately, we were unable to solve this case on our own and are in desperate need of your assistance. I apologize for my incompetence."

After gazing at me for a few moments, Ranpo lets out a sigh.

"Well...... Ah, fine, I *guess* I'll lend you a hand! And there's nothing to be sorry about, Kunikida. If there's anyone to blame, it should be me for being too gifted! After all, *Super Deduction* is the greatest skill in the world, so coming to me for help is only natural!" With a boisterous laugh, he pats me on the shoulder.

"You are absolutely right." I wholeheartedly agree.

"K-Kunikida, are you okay? You don't have to hold it in," Dazai timidly says. *Hold what in...? What is he talking about? I'm perfectly fine.*

"Dazai, give Ranpo the files."

"Oh, sure. Hey, I'm the new guy, Osamu Dazai. Nice to meet you."

"Yes, I've heard a lot about you. I'm counting on you to find a good case. I'll be the one to solve it, of course."

Ranpo's eyes are locked on Dazai as he takes the documents.

"So, newbie. Uh...Dazai, was it? Where did you work prior to coming here?"

"Hmm?"

Ranpo's expression has faded, his eyes peering into Dazai's as if he is searching for something.

"I didn't really do anything after finishing school. Was just kinda around, you know?"

A few seconds go by as Ranpo silently stares at Dazai. Finally...

"Oh, that's nice. Anyway, welcome to the agency."

And that's it. He begins laying out the documents across the desk as if nothing happened. What was that just now?

"Dazai, what was that about?"

"Don't ask me... By the way, what kind of skill user is Ranpo?"

Oh, right, I still haven't explained it to him yet.

"Ranpo's *Super Deduction* gives him the incredible ability to deduce the truth about a case just by looking at it."

"What?! Is there really a skill like that?!"

It seems even Dazai can hardly believe it.

"Yes, and there are a lot of important people in the police and government officials who come to Ranpo every time they need help with a difficult case. His skill is what keeps this detective agency in business."

"I dunno, it's just hard to believe a skill like that actually exists." He doesn't appear convinced.

"You'll believe it when you see it."

"Kunikida! Do you just need to know where the bomb is?"

"Yes. We're almost out of time. Finding that bomb is our top priority. We'll be able to disarm it if we know where it is."

"So I don't need to find this Alamta fellow, yes?"

"The bomb comes first."

"Okay, then let's get started! Ha-ha-ha! Sorry, everybody, it looks like your assistance won't be needed anymore now that I'm on the case. Dazai, hand me those glasses."

Ranpo puts on the black-framed glasses that Dazai hands him. Putting them on is apparently needed to activate his skill. His eyes sharpen into a radiant gaze that could pierce through all of nature, and his mind becomes an oracle of the gods.

————*Super Deduction.*

"..I've got it."

Ranpo sets his glasses down.

"Wait. Seriously?"

Dazai, standing behind Ranpo, holds his breath as he leans forward in curiosity.

"Map."

Ranpo points. I get the large map of Yokohama from the bookshelf, then spread it out over the desk. Where did this maniac—an apostle of panic and fear—hide this weapon of pure evil and mass destruction? At a train station? A major hospital? A school? Perhaps a skyscraper, even? Or is it at city hall? What about a shopping mall? The worst-case scenarios pop into my mind, one after another.

"The bomb is..."

I wait with bated breath as Ranpo lowers his finger over the map.

"...right here. *This fishing-gear shop.*"

.................................What?

A fishing-gear shop?

I must be hearing things. Perhaps there's a secret facility here? Or maybe they deal in illegal goods?

"...I see," Dazai mutters to himself after a few moments go by. "That's it... That's it! Ranpo's skill is real! If you're going to set a bomb, this fishing-gear shop is the only place that makes sense! Kunikida, we have to hurry!"

"I see the new guy's blown away by how amazing I am."

"I am! That was incredible! You are without a doubt an extraordinary detective! I'm so glad I joined this agency! Now come on! We don't have time to waste, Kunikida! We'll be able to make it before sundown if we leave now!"

"But, Dazai, I..."

"I'll explain on the way! Hurry!"

"Good luck, you two!"

With Dazai dragging me by the sleeve, I reluctantly leave the detective agency behind.

We get into the company car and head straight toward the fishing-gear shop.

Since I prefer not to ride in a murder box on wheels, I decide to drive.

"Now tell me what's going on, Dazai," I say to him.

"Sure, I'll explain, but you're not doubting Ranpo's deduction, right?"

"If Ranpo says the bomb is in the fishing-gear shop, then it's in the fishing-gear shop. I still don't get why you believed him, though."

Ranpo has the ability to see the truth, and his *Super Deduction* has never let us down. But there's something bugging me about Dazai being so easily convinced.

"It's simple when you look at the map."

I visualize the map in my head. The only things around the fishing-gear shop are roads, corporate facilities, and small shops. While there would be a fair number of victims, it lacks the viciousness one would expect from an international terrorist.

"Stop testing me. I have plenty of other things I need to think about. Just tell me what's going on."

"I thought about it after checking out the files we had on Alamta. He's been behind multiple large-scale bombings around the world, but he never bombs the same place twice. He's already bombed a luxury hotel packed with tourists, a military communications office, and a skyscraper's support beams. He always chooses an area that would produce the most damage to his target. So what area is he targeting this time?"

"Quit playing games and tell me."

"Alamta's target is...the oil storage facilities."

A bolt of lightning shoots down my spine as if I've been hit in the head with a hammer.

The petroleum complex in Yokohama!

How did I not think of that? Yokohama, Japan's most prominent port city, is the largest hub for transporting fuel by sea. There is a sizable plot of land at the port with numerous facilities that store oil and natural gas. Day and night, enormous amounts of fuel are carried out from those facilities to support industries throughout the Kanto region. Furthermore, the complex is surrounded by factories that use petrochemical-based materials, steel production factories, and petroleum production factories. If an explosion was to happen around the petroleum complex and the storage tanks caught fire, then the entire port would be engulfed in flames before long. The fire would most likely last for days, resulting in the worst industrial disaster this country has ever seen. Petrochemical fires are difficult to put out with water, which would even further prolong the destruction done. Not only would human lives be lost, but the domestic economy would suffer immeasurable damage as well.

"I see. So you were so impressed with Ranpo because of how accurate his deduction was."

"No, that's not why."

What?

"What amazed me was neither the novel idea of targeting an oil storage facility nor Ranpo's skill."

"Then what was it?"

"Heh-heh. What surprised me the most was the fact that *Ranpo's 'skill' isn't actually a skill at all.*"

...Huh?

"Don't be ridiculous. As if someone without a skill could really do something like that."

"That's what makes it so amazing! Listen to this. When Ranpo was thinking, I sneaked up behind him and pinched some of his hair."

"What?"

Dazai was indeed standing behind Ranpo the entire time, now that I think about it. But when did he—?

"As you know, I can nullify people's abilities just by touching them. I guess you could call me an anti-skill user. As long as I'm touching someone—no matter how powerful they may be—they will be unable to use their skill. So what I'm trying to say is…"

Ranpo's *Super Deduction* isn't a skill?

"Then that means—"

"It's just simple *deduction*. He reached a theoretical conclusion in the blink of an eye based on his own observations and inferences. He linked his knowledge on disasters, the files on Alamta, and the map of Yokohama to come to a conclusion in a matter of seconds. It was like I was watching a great detective from a novel find out who was behind the crime— Wait. No, it was more like watching the famous detective at the end of a novel after solving all the cases. Without leaving the building or meeting the suspect, Ranpo figured out where the bomb was simply by glancing at the files we gave him. He possesses tremendous deductive and observational skills that your average fictional detective could only dream of."

Deduction? What he's doing is not a skill or a supernatural phenomenon but purely the product of thought?

"But is that even possible? I mean, how…?"

"That's what impressed me. A skill would make this just another phenomenon, which wouldn't even be surprising, let alone impressive. But Ranpo is utilizing his brain, something we all have, to reach these conclusions. So Alamta disappeared two days ago, thus probably not having enough time to obtain a permit to get into the oil storage facilities or disguise himself as a worker there. The easiest thing he could've done was use cash to rent a car, store the bomb in it, park it somewhere near the oil storage facilities, and leave it there. If the explosive's effective casualty range is around six hundred fifty feet, then that would leave within that range only the shops that have an oil storage tank, and the only place at the port that meets these conditions is..."

"The fishing-gear shop."

"Exactly. Of course, things like wind direction and how difficult it would be to discover the bomb are also factors, but... Wow! I still can't believe how Ranpo figured that out just by looking at the documents we gave him. That guy's got some serious powers of deduction and observation! And even Ranpo himself seems to think he's using a skill. Man, that is one amazing detective. I need to start applying myself more."

I finally understand why Dazai was so impressed. No matter how divine it may be, a skill is nothing more than a bewildering phenomenon. However, things are different if these powers of deduction are something the person possesses on their own. Ranpo has solved far more than a few dozen cases in the past, to say the least, and he solved them in an instant with only a small amount of information. Not once has he been wrong. Calling what he does a superhuman feat still wouldn't be enough to illustrate how unbelievable it truly is—an ability that surpasses all skills. I could only describe it as a divine skill rarely seen in Japan—no, in the entire world.

Still, though...

I look over at Dazai in the passenger seat.

"I've never seen you marvel over someone else's skills like that before."

"Huh? Really? Lots of things take me by surprise. Like, once, I tried to pick up a clam with my chopsticks, and it was still alive. I was so startled, I nearly—"

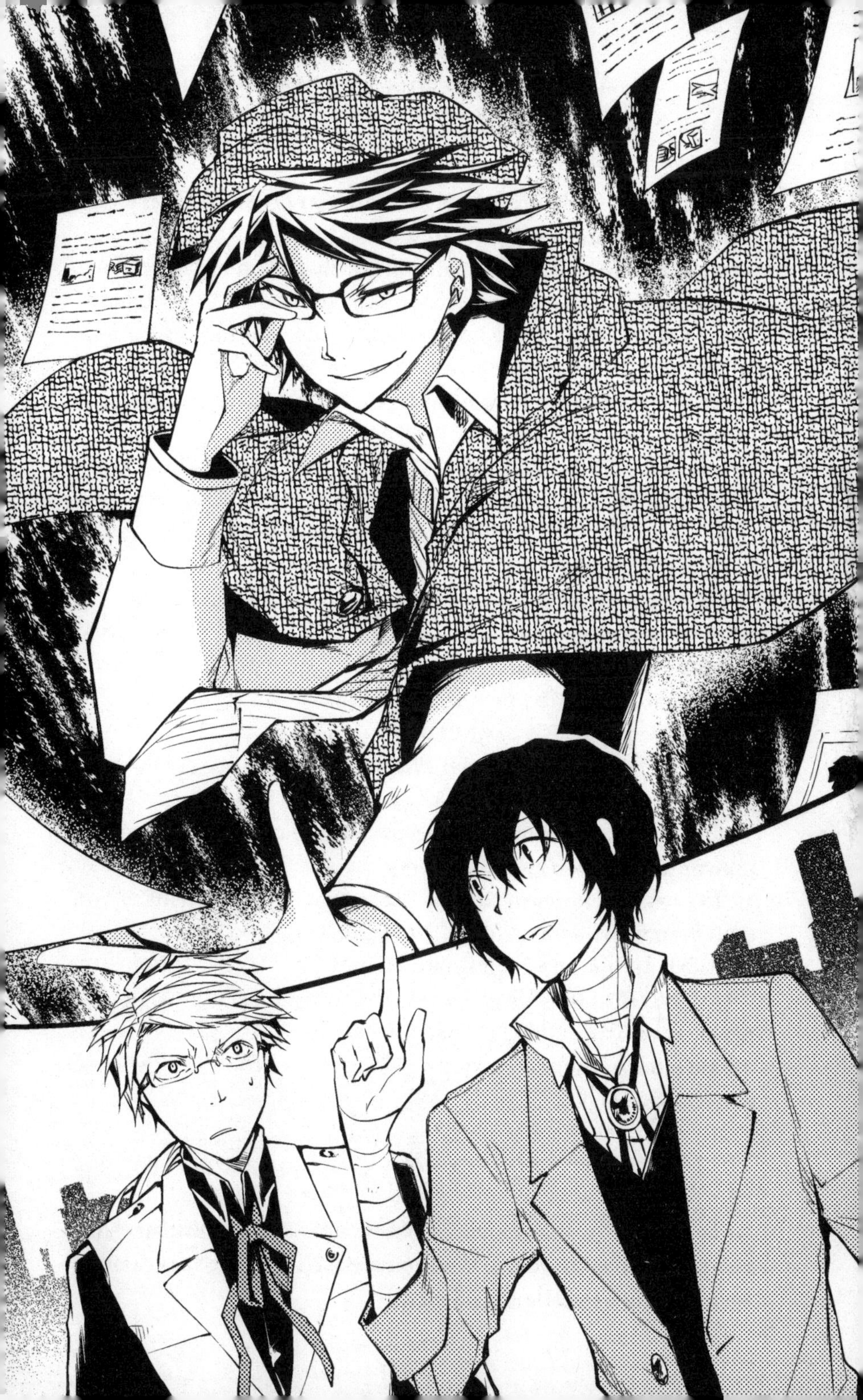

"That's not what I'm talking about. You seemed taken aback that someone had the ability to see and know all."

For someone so full of eccentricities, there is something about his behavior that makes it seem as if he has an unobstructed view of the world. I don't know exactly why, but all his emotions strike me as an act to some degree. Is he just playing dumb? Could there be more to him than he's letting on, lurking behind his ambiguous mannerisms?

"I guess. But you, Kunikida, I've got a good idea of who you are now, so nothing you do will ever surprise me. I mean, compared with me, you're just a simple man with a simple mind, after all."

"What did you just say?!"

"See? You wear your heart on your sleeve. You don't hide how you're really feeling. It's nice. You know what else is nice? Just knowing that you're going to be worrying later to yourself, 'Am I really that simple?'"

"Why, you—"

But I refrain from arguing. Whatever my response, he's just going to end up telling me, "I knew you'd say that."

"One day, you will be amazed by what I am capable of, and I guarantee you won't see it coming."

"I'm looking forward to it. I'll take you out for a drink if you end up surprising me."

"All right, it's a deal. You better not forget."

"I won't. Besides, I've got nothing to lose either way. Oh, look, I can see the fishing-gear shop."

I slow down the car and park on the side of the street where I can see the shop.

○ ○ ○

After getting out of the car, I observe the store. Only an hour remains before sundown. We should have the bomb disarmed in time as long as nothing goes wrong.

"Any idea what kind of car we're looking for?"

"It's simple, really. Just look for a large commercial vehicle with tinted windows to keep people from seeing inside."

I park the company car slightly away, then carefully approach the shop. I cannot deny the possibility that there might be armed personnel hiding somewhere in order to protect the bomb.

The fishing-gear shop seems to be closed for the day, so only a few cars sparsely occupy the parking lot, which could fit a little over ten vehicles. There's no sign of anyone in the parking area, and the slope on the west side leaves the whole place dim. I turn my head until I find a bunch of tall oil storage tanks behind me reaching out as far as the port itself. The closest tank is only around three hundred feet away from me. If the parking lot was to be blown up, the hellish flames would undoubtedly spread across every tank with ease.

"Kunikida, check that car out."

I face the direction Dazai is pointing in, where I find a small white commercial vehicle parked with a rental car plate. The tinted windows are visible even from afar. Furthermore, the car seems to be sitting lower than the others even though nobody is inside, which suggests it's not totally empty. I jot WIRELESS JAMMER down in my notebook before tearing the page out and focusing. Then the sheet of paper instantly transforms into a handheld wave inhibitor.

"Dazai, place this by the vehicle but keep your eye out for booby traps. I'm going to search the vicinity."

The jammer bears a strong resemblance to a cell phone. However, this device can intervene with radio channels, making nearby wireless devices unable to communicate with one another. It has an effective radius of around fifteen feet. The bomber won't be able to remotely detonate the bomb with this nearby.

I grip my gun while scouting around the parking area. I keep my guard up, but there are no signs of any snipers or enemies waiting to ambush. Instead, I find two recording devices hidden in the grass. One camera is the same type we found at the abandoned hospital, while the other is a smaller wireless type. This only further confirms that the bomb is here.

Suddenly, I hear people's voices and lift my head.

—*What's going on?*

People have started to gather on the other side of the road. Around ten people appear to be surrounding something, their faces clouded with worry. I have a bad feeling about this. After hiding my gun, I approach the crowd. Then I cut my way through to get a look at the cause of all this fuss.

My breath catches in my throat. There's something there that shouldn't be.

It's Alamta's body.

"Hey, Kunikida, I placed the jammer by the car. What do you want me to—?"

Dazai calls out to me from over my shoulder, but even he finds himself at a loss for words at the sight.

Why is this guy here?

Why is he dead?

I approach the corpse. There are no signs of hypostasis and no postmortem rigidity in the chin. He is still warm under the arms. It's evident that he was killed only moments ago—murdered right before we arrived. Not only that, but there are no visible wounds on the body. Nor are there any external changes that might indicate how he died. Instead, countless black symbols appear on his skin, covering his body like blemishes: "00." Two zeros? Are these tattoos? Or could this be—?

"Kunikida, the military's bomb squad will be here soon. Let's let them handle the technical stuff and get out of here." Dazai places a hand on my shoulder.

"......Okay."

I checked Alamta's belongings, but all he had was some change and a fake license—nothing of use. And with the mystery left unsolved, Dazai and I plow through the growing crowd of spectators and leave the scene.

⬡ ⬡ ⬡

I ruminate behind the wheel of the company car.

Why did Alamta have to die? And who wanted him dead?

"Kunikida, I get that thinking is important, but make sure to watch where you're driving, too, okay?" Dazai says from the passenger seat.

"I know," I tell him as I grip the steering wheel.

This situation needs analyzing. On the surface, there are but two cases here: the Yokohama kidnappings and the bomber. The perpetrators were the taxi driver and Alamta, respectively. That much is clear. But there's another common motive between these two cases: damaging the detective agency's name by releasing to the public footage of our failure to save the victims. The cabdriver and Alamta are most likely not involved with this goal, though. Someone must have been manipulating them from behind the scenes.

That someone is the Azure Apostle.

This person manipulated both the taxi driver and Alamta and made them the perpetrators. And just like that, the Azure Apostle attacked the detective agency without getting their own hands dirty by making it look like the other two committed these crimes of their own accord.

Attacking them is next to impossible, since they gave so few orders and simply let the perpetrators do as they pleased. Both the cabdriver and the bomber committed the crimes on their own turf in their own way. Perhaps they didn't even realize they were being used as pawns. If we don't stop the one behind all this, then it won't be long before we are attacked for a third time, something the agency might not be able to handle. The clues we have are next to nothing, though, which leaves me puzzled as to how we're going to find this mastermind.

There's one more thing I'm worried about. What is the Azure Apostle going to be charged with? The only crimes they've committed are secretly videoing and threatening us. They didn't kill anybody or blow up anything, and our chances of building a case to get them charged for instigating murder and kidnapping are extremely slim. Should I just hope the Azure Apostle accidentally left some evidence behind at the scene of the crime? And yet—

That's when my cell phone begins to ring. It's the detective agency's president. I pull over on the side of the road and press the call button.

"Kunikida, my informant in the military just contacted me. The taxi driver... He's dead."

What?!

"But wasn't he midflight on one of the military police's aircrafts?"

"He was. During questioning, he suddenly began suffering intense pain and passed not long after. His cause of death is unknown, but I was told two black zeros started to surface all over his body... Get back to the agency and let's go carefully over the situation."

The phone clicks. My head is swimming with questions.

Our sole path to the Azure Apostle has been cut. The only clue we had to locate this person was to find out who taught that driver about the organ trade, but those tracks died along with him. It's almost as if the Azure Apostle is watching us, always one step ahead. Alamta was killed right before we arrived at the scene, and now the cabdriver, our last hope, is gone as well. Just who is this person? The enemy is somebody who knows everything about the detective agency's investigation and every move we make. Somebody who can constantly tamper with the scene of the crime and manipulate the situation from afar.

"You okay, Kunikida? You look real tense."

I don't even have a moment to respond. How is the enemy getting inside info? How are they always a step ahead of the detective agency? My cell phone rings once more, interrupting my train of thought. It's Rokuzo.

"Hey, Four-Eyes. Got a moment?"

"What is it?"

"It's... It's about the e-mail you asked me to trace. I did it."

"What?!"

That's it. The sender of that threatening e-mail said their name was the Azure Apostle, and they gave orders to investigate the kidnapping and bombing. If we can find out where that e-mail came from...

"I'll cut to the chase. Both e-mails came from the same computer, which was heavily protected. But hey, I was able to break through. Anyway—"

"Who're you talking to, Kunikida?"

I raise my hand, cutting Dazai off. "Go on."

"All you asked me to do was trace the e-mail, so don't come to me with questions about what it means, okay? 'Cause I ain't gonna know. So with that in mind—"

"Get on with it."

"Okay, fine, I'll tell ya. So...

"...those e-mails were sent from inside the detective agency... from the computer of the new guy—Dazai."

————————————————————————Come again?

My brain freezes over, my mind completely blank.

This can't be. It has to be some sort of trap. Dazai's been with me the entire time investigating the...

—The enemy is somebody who knows everything about the detective agency's investigation and every move we make. Somebody who can constantly tamper with the scene of the crime and manipulate the situation from afar.

"I'll call you back." I hang up the phone.

"What was that about? It sounded like you were talking to Rokuzo."

"Just shut up for a moment."

My thoughts are scattered.

Dazai. Osamu Dazai, a newcomer at the detective agency who popped up out of nowhere.

This sequence of events started after he showed up.

"I asked a close acquaintance in the military's intelligence department to do a background check on him, but eerily, they found nothing.

"It's as if someone very carefully wiped his background clean."

The poison gas at the abandoned hospital was triggered when Dazai touched the trap while we were trying to save the kidnapped victims…and yet, for some reason, he wasn't in any of the released footage.

How was he able to stay clear of the cameras?

A clever and cautious string puller, the Azure Apostle never soils their own hands.

Someone of considerable intellect, whose acting abilities could deceive even embassy staff, with knowledge of the organ trade…

I start the car engine and begin driving again.

"Dazai."

"Yeah?"

"Let's go for a drive."

◇ ◇ ◇

I turn the steering wheel, entering a deserted mountain path and continuing down it until we reach an old abandoned storehouse.

"What's this?" Dazai asks while looking at the storage shed.

"It's a storehouse I used for work once. At one time, it was used for industrial materials, but it was abandoned after the company moved overseas. Nobody comes here anymore, which makes it the perfect place to discuss things in private."

"Oh, great."

A lukewarm reply. I drive inside the storehouse and park. Since the building still has all four walls, I don't have to worry about being watched, and I would be able to hear any reinforcements should they come.

"Get out."

Without a word, Dazai gets out of the car. Before I do the same, I open my automatic pistol's magazine to make sure it's loaded. Then, after writing in my notebook, I exit the vehicle as well.

"Gee, it sure is quiet here. Definitely the perfect place if you ever wanted to talk in secret. So why are we—?"

I point the pistol at Dazai.

"...What's the gun for?"

"Take a guess."

"Hold on, Kunikida. I thought you hated jokes like this."

"I do. But this isn't a joke."

"This must have something to do with that phone call, right? Well, whatever you heard, I'm sure it's all some kind of misunderstanding. I'd be able to explain myself if you just told me what he said."

"I hope so." I tighten my finger around the trigger. "When the victims at the abandoned hospital were gassed, you were somehow able to avoid showing your face in the footage. Why is that?"

"That's it?" Dazai looks troubled. "I just happened to see the surveillance equipment when I walked into the room. I was going to tell you, but we found the victims almost immediately after, so I didn't get the chance. That's why I didn't say anything. I apologize—"

"Really? Are you sure you didn't know where the cameras were and what they were for from the start?" I continue to press him. "Next question. You were the one who suggested we go to the embassy in order to find the bomber. How were you able to come up with that idea so quickly? Was it because you knew about Alamta beforehand, perhaps?"

"Oh, come on. You're joking, right? You should be praising me for my acumen, not doubting me. Is that what all this is about?"

"Where did you learn about the organ-trafficking syndicate?"

"That's... Listen, I told you already. I was at the pub..."

"You can't come up with a better lie than that? Was it just a coincidence that you ran into Chief Taneda, head of the Special Division for Unusual Powers?"

"W-wait! C'mon, Kunikida. Could you put the gun down? I'll tell you everything after you do that."

"Why were the Azure Apostle's e-mails sent from your computer?! Answer me!" I yell, cocking the pistol's hammer. Dazai's face goes blank.

"I see. So that's what Rokuzo told you on the phone, huh? He's a real talented kid... I'm sure he'll make a great detective one day." His tone is flat, his face void of all emotion.

Thinking back, there was always something enigmatic about Dazai. While he struck me as an eccentric, he also perfectly expressed the kinds of schemes and knowledge necessary to influence others. Just as his excellent acting at the embassy fooled everybody, who's to say that this Dazai persona isn't just an act as well?

"Convince me of your innocence right now, or I'll shoot."

"You can't shoot me." He shakes his head. "You're conscientious and an idealist. You unravel all the mysteries, get the criminal to confess, then arrest them and have them tried by the law. That's what's ideal to you. You would never kill the suspect somewhere like this while the truth is still up in the air."

"The law is powerless against the Azure Apostle." Even if I demand he be prosecuted, there's no case against someone who didn't kill or kidnap anybody, let alone instigate another to do so. It's a lost cause. "I'll shoot if that's what must be done."

—*If you sense any signs of wickedness in his heart, shoot him.*" The president's words... The heavy pistol I was entrusted with...
—*Do what must be done.*"

"Kunikida, hypothetically speaking, let's say I am the Azure Apostle, and let's say your ideals dictate that you should hurry up and kill me... Even then, you still couldn't shoot me." There's a cold-blooded, inhuman glow in his eyes, as if he can see right through everything—as if he knows all. "Think back to when you found Alamta's body. All he had on him was some change and a fake license, which begs the question: *What happened to the detonator?*"

The detonator could be used to wirelessly set off the bomb, but there's no threat without it.

"Whoever's really behind all this has it."

"Exactly. And what if that person knew every move the detective agency was making? And what if that person knew that the detective agency figured out where the bomb was? Don't you think they would have moved the bomb or prepared a spare?"

The next thing I know, Dazai's right hand is in his overcoat pocket. I'm not able to check if he's holding something from where I'm standing, though. Is he insinuating that there's still a bomb out there and that he has the detonator to it? Is that why he said I couldn't shoot him?

—*How naive.*

"I suspected as much, which is why I came prepared. Take a look at this."

I take *this* out of my breast pocket before placing it on the ground. "It's a wireless jammer just like the one I used before. No wireless devices can be used within fifteen feet of me. A detonator is no exception."

"Wha—?" Dazai's expression is overcome with surprise. My gun still aimed at him, I stick my hand into his pocket and feel something, then pull it out.

It's a fountain pen and a blue cloth.

"Looks like I couldn't fool you. Too bad it's just an ordinary fountain pen." Dazai cheerfully grins. It's the same pen he showed the receptionist at the embassy, the one he claimed was his favorite or something.

"Anyone else would have believed you, but it's going to take a little more than that to fool your partner."

I unscrew the pen top and take it off, revealing not an ink cartridge but a long, thin electrical device with an exposed circuit. It's a small transceiver.

"Is this the detonator?"

"...I'm impressed, Kunikida. Nothing gets by you, does it? Incredible." His smile is cold, inhuman. "I'm so glad you were my partner."

Those words have me boiling.

"Shut up!"

I point the pistol down and shoot, sending a bullet into the floor by his feet. Dazai doesn't even bat an eye.

"What do you want?! Why did you threaten the detective agency?! What was the point of killing the missing people and setting the bomb?! You... You were..."

You were so talented.

I couldn't have asked for a better partner.

"This is my final warning. Tell me everything, or I'll shoot."

Who is he? Who is the Azure Apostle? He has others do his

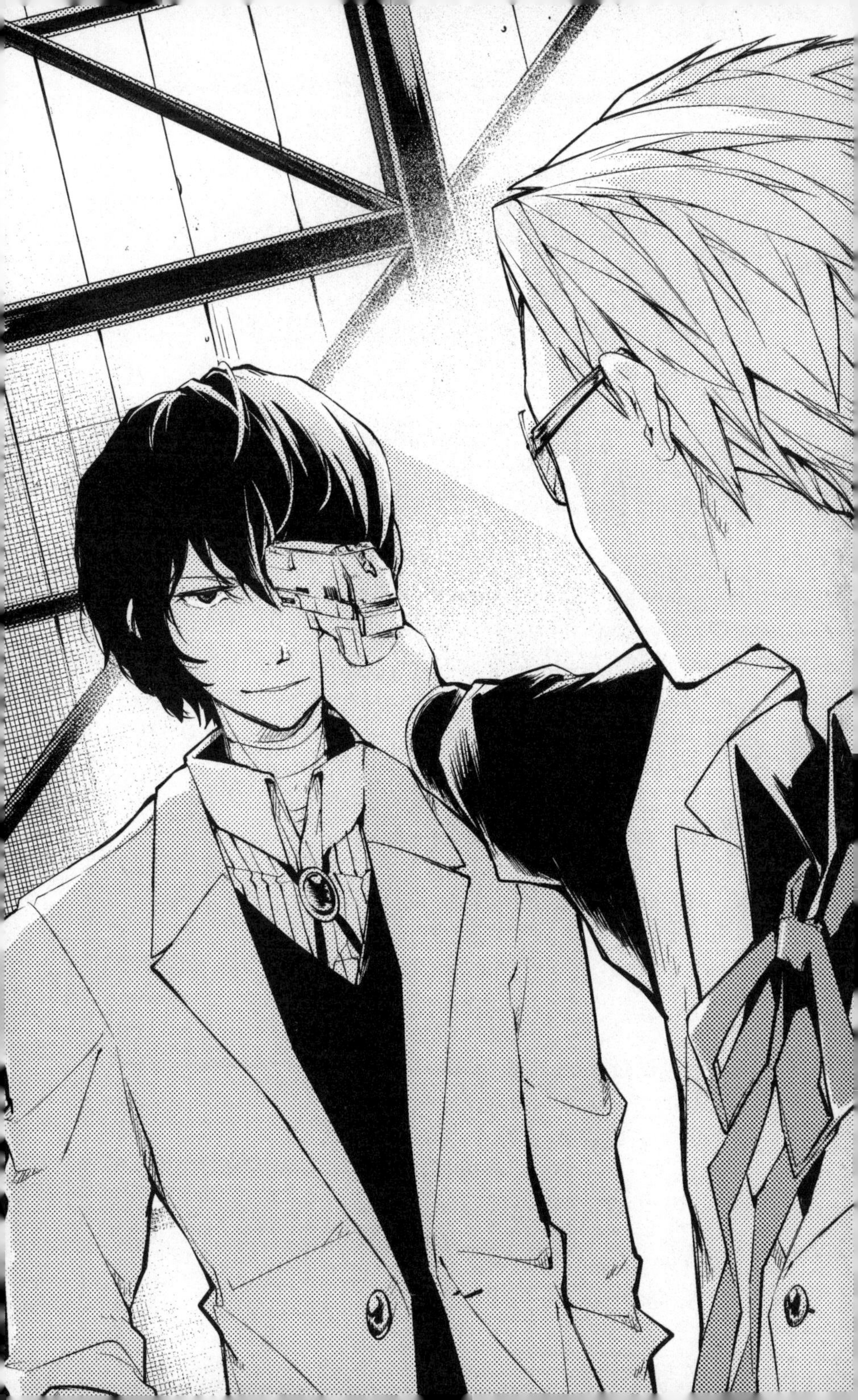

bidding before disposing of them without so much as lifting a finger...all while getting the victims involved as well.

Kill the criminal—

—*"Then let us realize an ideal world..."*

—*"Not by the hand of a god but by our own imperfect blood-stained hands."*

It can't be.

I glance at the blue cloth I swiped from Dazai's pocket. Have I seen something like this recently?

—*"I heard they never found the Azure King's body, either."*

—*"What if he faked his death to escape and is now in hiding somewhere?"*

We know who the Azure King was. He used to be a high-ranking government official. However, changing one's face or background isn't impossible with the help of a specialist. Even fooling the military police's forensics unit and faking one's death isn't entirely unfathomable. Could it be that...?

—*"We looked into his past but found nothing. It's completely blank."*

Then could Dazai be...?

"Are you— Are you the Azure King? Was this grand scheme of yours all just to get back at the detective agency?"

"Shoot me."

He grins mirthfully from ear to ear. There's tranquility in his smile.

"You win, Kunikida. Shoot me. You must have received orders to, yes? This is how it should be, and you have every right to."

"What do you mean I have 'every right'?!"

"I wouldn't mind being shot by you."

No. This isn't what I want. I want to hear the truth. I want Dazai to tell me the truth.

—*"However, if you sense any signs of wickedness in his heart..."*

No. I must find the truth.

—*"Shoot him."*

* * *

"I wouldn't mind being shot by you"?

I see.
It all makes sense now.

"Understood."
I lift the pistol, aligning the sight just between his eyebrows. Tucking my arms in, I close one eye while carefully aiming. There is no way to miss from this distance.
"I'm going to shoot, Dazai. I'm really going to do it, so if you're going to panic, you better start now."
His peaceful smile never once wavers.
"Shoot me," he says.

There is no longer any hesitation in his words. I bend my index finger around the trigger, and a bullet spits out of the muzzle.

The bullet tears through the air until it hits him right between the eyes. Dazai's head flies back, causing his spine to arch backward. Knocked off his feet, he flies into the air and then—
—he hits the ground.

I lower my pistol. White gunpowder faintly drifts from the muzzle.
"……"
Perfect accuracy: The bullet hit him right in the middle of his skull. There was no way I'd miss this close. After putting the safety back on, I check the pistol to make sure there won't be any misfires before returning the weapon to my pocket. I crush the fountain pen–shaped detonator in my hand, bending and twisting it until it can no longer function.
I have to think about my next move. I begin to walk back to the parked car. After taking a few steps, my cell phone starts to ring.

I seem to be out of the wireless jammer's range now. Expressionless, I look down at the screen. It's the detective agency.

"Yes?"

It's Dr. Yosano.

"Kunikida? Listen, we just got another threat from that obnoxious Azure Apostle guy! I'm sending it to you right now, so get a move on!"

"But I'm—"

The call ends, and I get a notification telling me I've received an e-mail. I open my in-box to display the following message:

Dear Sir,

I am contacting you to discuss a third request. Passenger airline flight JA815S is currently midflight. I have taken the liberty of sending an interference signal to the aircraft's engine and yoke that will disable their functions. I would like for you to remove the device from the aircraft and save the passengers.

Thank you for your understanding.

Yours sincerely,
The Azure Apostle

"An airplane...?"

Another threat? Now?

Preventing an aircraft attack presents a far greater challenge than a kidnapping or bomb. Trying to hop on a high-speed airplane midflight to remove some device is beyond the realm of possibility. I would need a military fighter aircraft to even consider it. No, I still wouldn't be able to get in if the passenger plane had some sort of system to prevent intrusion.

While shutting down the engine and control wheel would indeed cut the plane's power, it would still be able to glide for a short while. But even then, without the power to steer, there would be nothing preventing the plane from suddenly dropping before its inevitable crash. Without control, it would be difficult to land in a relatively safe location such as the ocean, and if the plane hits the ground, then everyone on the plane will die, barring a miracle more awesome than the creation of the universe itself.

There's only one way to end this seemingly inescapable disaster.

I glance at Dazai. He's lying on his back with his eyes closed. Then I slowly approach him.

⬡ ⬡ ⬡

"How long do you plan on playing dead? Get up. We've got work to do." I kick his body.

"Hmm? Aw, c'mon, just a few more minutes." Dazai pouts.

⬡ ⬡ ⬡

"Something happen?"

"Yeah, we got another e-mail from the real enemy threatening a plane crash, so if you're not the person behind this, get up and help."

"I knew you would use *that* to shoot me, Kunikida." Dazai grins, still on his back.

"Same as ever, I see. You are free to scheme all you want, but don't involve me in your ridiculous skits."

I take the pistol I shot earlier and toss it at Dazai. He catches it, and almost instantly, *it transforms back into a piece of note-book paper in his hands.*

"But how did you know? I received a pistol just like it from the director. What made you so sure I wouldn't shoot you with that one?"

"Because I trust you, of course. Someone as cautious as you wouldn't threaten a person with a real gun out of the blue like that."

"Hearing you say the word *trust* really tarnishes the word."

The pistol I shot Dazai with was one I created out of a sheet of paper using *The Matchless Poet*. Since the bullets were also created using my skill, they were nullified and vaporized by Dazai's own skill on contact.

"When did you first realize it?"

"When you told me to shoot you."

Dazai would never say, "I wouldn't mind being shot by you." One thing I learned while working with him is that nine times out of ten, he's messing with someone when he says hackneyed phrases like that. Under normal circumstances, he would have said, "Now I can finally die," while dancing and jumping for joy.

"Oh, and one more thing. This pen of yours—this isn't a detonator. It's a covert listening device, isn't it?"

"Quite so."

I haven't been working as a detective all this time just for show. I can tell whether something's a detonator. That little charade of his was to get me to block the bug. He predicted I would bring a jammer and use it.

"When were the fountain pens swapped?"

"You know when we were by the fishing-gear shop? Well, someone switched the pens on me when I was pushing through the crowd. Ugh. That really *was* my favorite pen, y'know. They'll be sorry when I make them reimburse me. It was really hard to write with, though."

"So that must have been when they put that azure banner in your pocket, too."

The enemy was planning on framing Dazai as the mastermind behind this string of events, but we were one step ahead of them.

"But I know you. You wouldn't let the enemy just brush by you when you knew they were coming, right?"

"Of course not. In fact, I'd been playing the villain for a good while just for this moment. I waited for the moment they bugged me to place a GPS tracker on them. They were fools to believe they could ever outwit me."

Dazai knew what the enemy was trying to do and still went along with their scheme. A criminal like the Azure Apostle always needs others to do their dirty work. The kidnappings, the bomb—every criminal act was outsourced, every event carefully planned to avoid suspicion. So why not outsource the role of "Azure Apostle" to someone else as well? And Dazai figured it out.

"It first hit me when the victims were gassed at the abandoned hospital because *I never touched the electric lock on that cage*, and yet, gas started to spray out from who knows where. Which means the enemy was watching us and controlling the poison-gas device remotely to make it look like I did it. I thought, 'Why would they do that?' That's when I started to feel something was up, and it wasn't long before I figured out what they were trying to do."

The enemy's objective was to *frame* someone, and who better than a newcomer with an unknown past? Dazai, however, didn't take any steps to prevent that from happening, either.

"This villain we're up against never reveals themselves. We have no evidence to identify them, and they've thoroughly made sure they can't be traced. Even so, this person still has to come in contact with the outside world from time to time, and that's when they make their puppets. The only people lucky enough to meet the Azure Apostle, albeit briefly, are the perpetrators like the cabdriver and bomber: the ones who actually carry out the crimes. So my only chance of coming into contact with this guy was becoming a criminal myself, and if you hadn't realized that, I would've been locked away in the criminal's place."

That's why Dazai continued to pretend he didn't know he was being set up until he could destroy the listening device in a natural way. From the point of view of our eavesdropping enemy, the bug no longer functioning is not a problem. They probably believe that everything is going according to plan.

A brief taste of freedom from the enemy's watch—Dazai didn't tell me what was really going on and continued to play the villain just to create this moment for us.

I am once against struck with admiration.

The man is incredible.

Our enemy has the wits and resources to manipulate a seasoned bomber. Simply being able to realize they're setting you up is an amazing feat itself. Dazai, however, worked their scheme into his own like a hook to drag out our foe.

"I bet the guy who planted the bug on me is laughing themselves silly right about now. They probably think their little plan worked and that I was killed by one of my own. This would also be the perfect moment for the enemy to make their next move."

I nod. It was probably no coincidence that the enemy waited for this moment to threaten us with the airplane. After listening to our conversation, they probably don't even doubt that Dazai was executed, and their assumption was *almost* a reality. They were waiting for Dazai to go down before sending in the third threat.

"This would've been the worst possible timing for the detective agency to get the threat. It's impossible to get inside a moving plane to remove that device. Plus, only moments ago, Kunikida killed me, the supposed author of said threats. The case would be sunk, and it'd be curtains for the agency."

He's right. If the scenario played out as the enemy had written it, then that is exactly what would have happened.

—And if it had been anyone other than Dazai, it probably would have worked.

"There is only one way we can do this... Follow the tracking device you placed on the enemy *to their hideout and put an end to this ourselves!*"

"Let's show this 'Azure Apostle' fellow who they're dealing with."

Dazai gets to his feet.

○ ○ ○

Leaving the bug and jammer in the abandoned storehouse, we get in the car and start our search. Dazai turns on his handheld transmitter, displaying the location of the tracking device. It's relatively close by in the mountains, and it's not moving. I'll have to ask the detective agency to gather information on the area. If this is where the enemy's hideout is, then I cannot deny the possibility of there being some sort of defense facility.

However, before that happens, the agency gets in touch with me and says they were contacted by someone on the plane. Apparently, somebody happened to find a video communication device while checking the passengers' belongings. The agency transfers the video call to my cell phone; I can see the cabin of the plane.

"I... I'm, um, one of the people on the airplane. Mommy w-wasn't feeling well...so I'm talking f-for her. The p-plane is falling...s-so fast... Everybody's c-crying and screaming..."

"Damn it!"

Speaking into the camera is a little girl no more than ten years old. Tears stream down her face as the aircraft rocks back and forth.

"The pilot t-told us to s-stay in our seats, b-but...but nobody's listening, and there are s-some people fighting..."

"I'm speaking to you from on the ground. Can you hear me? I know it's hard, but I need you to tell me what's going on in the plane right now."

"It's f-falling. They s-said the engine stopped moving...and th-the steering wheel d-doesn't work anymore, either."

Although clearly terrified, it seems the little girl understands what's going on. She desperately tries to describe the situation as best she can.

"Can you hear me? Are we...gonna d-die? E-everyone says we're gonna die... I'm scared... Mommy's not moving...or a-answering me. P-please, please help us..."

"Hello, little one. Can you hear me?" Dazai takes over the call. "We here are airplane experts. There's nothing to worry about anymore. We're going to fix the plane. What's your name, little miss?"

"Ch-Chiyo..."

"Chiyo, everything's going to be okay. Got any snacks with you?"

"Mommy gave me this piece of candy..."

"Candy, huh? I love candy, too. It's so sweet, and it really helps you relax, doesn't it?"

"Dazai—"

"I've got this... Chiyo, first, I want you to really take your time enjoying that piece of candy. After that, I'm going to need you to take that device you're talking into and bring it to the captain's room. Do you know where the captain's room is?"

Chiyo nods, wiping the tears from her eyes.

"Don't worry. There's nobody screaming in there, and I bet your mommy will be feeling better in no time."

"B-but I... I can't go alone. I can't leave Mommy behind..."

"Your mommy's gonna be just fine. The pilot will make things all better. So I'm going to need you to take that device to their room and give it to them, okay?"

The little girl stares at the floor for a few moments, then takes the candy out of her pocket and stands, albeit trembling. From there, she starts walking toward the cockpit. My hand tightens around the steering wheel.

"This is the captain of flight 815S. We are currently experiencing

engine failure and are unable to make contact with any control towers, so we've had to resort to internal navigation. Who am I speaking to?" The captain takes the call. He appears to be an experienced pilot a little over forty years old.

Facing the communicator, I reply, "We're with the Armed Detective Agency. The military's deployment forces won't make it in time, so we will be handling the situation. I need you to be specific about what's happening to the airplane."

"The Armed Detective Agency? ...You mean those detectives who let those missing people get killed? Just great. Just in case something happens to us—"

"Sorry to disappoint you, but we're the only ones who understand what's going on here. It would take several hours before the military could grasp the situation and orchestrate a rescue mission."

"We don't have 'several hours'! Nearly every electronic device on this plane has quit working, so we can't increase or decrease speed, let alone roll. If my calculations are correct, we have only an hour before we crash!"

"Listen to me. The airplane was purposefully sabotaged. Are there any strange devices on board? Or was anything destroyed?"

"...My copilot discovered a large iron box in the freight room. We found out that it was connected to some wires, but the iron box itself was welded to the aircraft. We wouldn't be able to move or destroy it with what we have available."

I see. The device must be interfering with the aircraft system. The enemy must have sneaked into a hangar where the aircraft was being stored, then welded a device that would temporarily paralyze the plane's control system. After takeoff, they must have remotely activated the device to prevent the aircraft from staying airborne.

I remember reading something similar to this for work once. The now-defunct National Defense Force had been developing equipment capable of crippling aircraft functions. Eventually, however, they learned that you would first have to carry the device onto the aircraft, so they abandoned the project. In spite of that, it bears a lot of similarities to this case. If the same type of device has been brought into this aircraft, then signals being sent from the ground are controlling interference. In short, cutting off the control unit's signal on the ground could very likely restore control on the aircraft.

"Captain, we are going to remove the source of the problem. I need you to be prepared to regulate the airplane's altitude when I give you the signal."

"Roger that. Just know that I won't be able to gain altitude if we get too close to the ground. I need you to hurry. We have four hundred and ten passengers on board, and according to my calculations, we have only an hour before we crash around Yokohama's designated tax haven."

Only an hour.

There most likely wouldn't be any survivors, regardless of how the plane crashes. To make matters worse, if it crashes in a densely populated industrial area such as the designated tax haven, then the damage it would bring would be devastating. Alamta's bomb would have been nothing compared with the disaster this would cause.

There's no time.

I step on the accelerator.

Following the tracker device, we race through the mountains of Yokohama. There's not a house in sight, and the rough bushlands cast shadows onto the car.

"Looks like this is it."

I stop the vehicle. Built into the mountain face is a black iron door. It leads to an air-raid shelter built during the war for the now-defunct National Defense Force. Never used, the crumbling military base has succumbed to the unforgiving flow of time.

I see now—shooting off a cannon inside wouldn't even catch anyone's attention, much less bring the device here.

That's when out of nowhere, the sound of gunfire assaults our ears from both sides. The company car shrieks as bullets rain down on it.

"We're under attack! Get out of the car!"

I slam on the gas and quickly accelerate before jumping out and escaping into the thickets.

"I guess this means we're at the right place...!"

The armed enemies are shooting at us with rifles from the lee of some slanted rocks. There are three...no, four of them.

"What do we do, Kunikida?!" Dazai shouts out while hiding in the shadow of a slope.

"They're only trying to buy time! I'll provide backup! Just get inside that building!"

Bullets fly over my head as I yell. I glance over at our attackers. All they're doing is firing at random and taking cover. Their guns are good quality, but they are not as experienced as the Port Mafia gangsters.

"The Matchless Poet: Flash Grenade!"

I've been using far too many pages out of my notebook lately!

I catapult the flash grenade, and the enemies recoil from the noisy explosion over their heads.

"Now's your chance! Go!" I urge Dazai while firing my weapon. He springs into action.

◊ ◊ ◊

Dazai separates from Kunikida and races through the decaying air-raid shelter. The tracker device's signal is coming from the maintenance depot on the other side. After climbing out of the pit, he passes through the marshaling yard before immediately dashing to the two-story maintenance depot's galvanized iron outer walls.

The abandoned maintenance depot has a hangar for storing cars and aircrafts on the first floor, with an operations room looking down at the hangar on the second floor. Dazai dashes up the staircase and rushes inside the operations room.

"It's here, huh?"

While the floors are discolored and worn with rust at every turn, the door's hinges appear to be new, implying someone has been frequently visiting this timeworn room. A near-empty liquor bottle rests on the table by a faintly smoking cigarette. The flashing light on the large communicator attached to the wall blinks, indicating it's still working.

Dazai is approaching the communicator when a shadow falls over him—a large foreign man now stands at his back. The muscle-bound, tanned individual with a tattoo of a camellia on his arm looks at Dazai in silence. Old scars run down his bald head and over his dark-green eyes.

"What are you doing here?" the giant barks.

"What am I doing here? ...Isn't it obvious?! I came to warn you!" Dazai swiftly turns around and shouts. "The Armed Detective Agency found our hideout! We've gotta get outta here, or we're all done for! Where's the boss? Come on—we don't have much time! They're gonna come breaking through the entrance any minute now!" He urgently rattles on without even taking a moment to breathe.

"I don't know you."

"Well, of course you don't. I work undercover for the boss. You know how secretive the guy is. Now hurry! Go get 'im!"

A hint of bewilderment flashes across the man's face.

"Okay."

He turns his back to Dazai to leave the operations room.

Crack.

The large man sluggishly falls to the ground. A large bump is forming on his head. Grinning, Dazai stands behind him with the bottle of liquor cracked in half in hand.

"The boss is a real secretive fellow. Not that I've ever met the guy, but it's just a hunch."

Having no more use for the bottle, Dazai tosses it to the floor before facing the communicator once more.

"All that's left is to send a stop signal with this."

⬡ ⬡ ⬡

I start to follow Dazai after neutralizing the enemy. In stark contrast with the shoot-out by the entrance, a dead silence hangs over the building's interior. Fresh footprints and tire tracks litter the ground, making it rather apparent this is their hideout. But I have no way of finding Dazai now. Plus, he has the transmitter's tracking device.

However, as I walk past the galvanized iron outer walls of a maintenance depot, I suddenly hear the sound of glass shattering coming from inside.

—*Is Dazai fighting with the enemy?*

Pressing my back against the wall, I get into stance with my pistol. I plunge through the entrance with the muzzle aimed inside, searching for the enemy. It appears the first floor was used for storing armored cars and aircrafts, but now it is nothing more than a vacant lot of exposed earth. I guess that leaves an office and the operations room for the second floor. If the communicator is anywhere, it would be on the second floor.

At that moment, I get a terrible feeling that something is wrong. A chill shoots down my spine, and it feels as if swarms of insects are crawling under my skin. Unable to endure it, I fall to my knees. That's when I notice some sort of patterns drawn into the ground: circles and lines along with various diagrams and letters. The illegible letters seem to be ancient symbols. It resembles a magic circle for rituals using a grimoire, but…my spine has been tingling with chills ever since I stepped on it. Which means—

I roll up my sleeve, an unbearable itching pain overtaking my arm.

The number "39" surfaces on my skin.

I check my entire body. Arms, chest, ankles: nine brands, resembling tattoos, cover me. I know for a fact these weren't there a few seconds ago.

"Gimme … Gimme your number."

I instinctively point my pistol in the direction of the fragile voice, where I find a boy—rather, a short young man—staggering in my direction. I aim my gun at him.

"Stop right there! We're with the Armed Detective—"

Before I can finish my sentence, I take an invisible blow from the side, which knocks me to the floor. I am slammed into the ground only to bounce back up and collide with the galvanized iron wall hard enough to warp it. My head is spinning, my vision swirling. I have no sense of balance after all that spinning from the hit. I have to fight back.

I'm somehow able to pick up my pistol lying on the ground by my side, but immediately, my arm is struck by another invisible blow that knocks it into the air and bends me backward. My bones creak as the pistol soars through the air.

"A feisty one, ain'tcha? How excellent. You must have a wonderful number."

The skinny young man picks up the pistol and curiously peeks into the muzzle.

Obviously he's a skill user, and one with a battle-oriented ability, at that. They appear to be some kind of long-range attacks. I look at the marking on my skin: the number "32."

Impossible—

"I'm impressed you found the place. That's the Armed Detective Agency for ya. That's the *amazing* Armed Detective Agency for ya."

The slender man points my gun in my direction, then empties the magazine until not a single bullet remains and the firing pin takes to the sky. The bullets pierce the ground before me.

"C'mon—I wouldn't shoot ya. It's a very important number, after all. I couldn't shoot ya."

A morbid smile runs across the slim figure's lips as he walks toward me.

"Every time you take damage, that number gets smaller. It even gets smaller as time passes. And when it reaches zero—"

"You... You're the skill user who killed the taxi driver and Alamta?"

"Heh-heh... Ha-ha... Ah-ha-ha-ha-ha! Oh, of *course* a detective would ask that. Ha-ha-ha!"

I fix my eyes on the young blond man dressed in a threadbare hooded jacket. Judging by appearance alone, he doesn't seem to have an aptitude for fighting. However, there is one thing I am sure of.

—*This skill user is the enemy's boss.*

⬡ ⬡ ⬡

Dazai operates the communicator.

"Yeesh, how old is this thing?! So if this is the frequency and this is the direction—"

A shadow moves behind him.

"It's no use! I can't input the final command— Hang on, do I need the control key to change the settings?!"

Colossal fists rain down from behind, smashing into Dazai's temple and spinning him across the floor like a rag doll. There's a dull thud when he collides with the desk.

"...That hurt, y'know."

Dazai stands, and his lips curl upward—a fierce grin—as fresh blood drips down his cheek.

The massive man slowly and emotionlessly approaches Dazai. On each hand are hammer-like steel knuckles. The man raises his arm in the air and swings once more, but Dazai kicks off the desk and dodges. In just one punch, the steel fist smashes the wooden desk into splinters.

"That's quite an arm you've got there! You really oughta consider working in freight delivery!"

Dazai slides across the floor to create some distance before facing the behemoth.

"Well, this is just no good. I'm quite weak, you see. A big guy like yourself would snap me right in two... But I promised Chiyo I would save her."

"I won't let you use...the communicator."

The man blocks the path to the device.

"Really? Guess I'll just give up and run away, then." Dazai swiftly turns around and bolts for the door.

"Get back here!"

As the giant man chases after him, Dazai races through the wooden door and closes it on his way out. Once the enemy reaches out to open the door, Dazai drop-kicks it from the other side, hitting his opponent in the process. Hampered by the door and unable to support the weight of Dazai's jump, the man is sent flying back. Fragments from the wooden door scatter as he rolls on the ground.

"Striiike!"

Upon landing, Dazai approaches the giant to follow up with another hit. The enemy swiftly goes for a sweep, seemingly unfazed by the kick, but Dazai leaps back as if he saw it coming.

"You're really tough! You know that?"

The man uses his back muscles to kick up off the ground, then throws a hook. Dazai manages to bob and weave out of the way, but part of his clothing catches on the steel knuckles just enough to pull him off-balance.

"Ack—"

A fist starts to bury into Dazai's stomach. He instantly jumps back to soften the blow, but the man's massive arm follows through until Dazai's body is thrown back by a punch strong enough to destroy a table. Doubled over, he soars straight into the wall on the other side of the room.

Blood and spittle drip from his mouth. The enemy raises his stout arm into the air and swings it like a club. Dazai rolls to his side to evade, but the man follows up with a backhand, knocking the detective's head so hard that his neck almost snaps as he is driven into the ground. Trembling, he staggers to his feet.

"Strong *and* fast, eh? ...What, were you raised by gorillas or something?"

While he may be joking, the sense of crisis in Dazai's eyes tells a different story:

—*I can't beat this guy.*

Dazai glances out the window at the storage room below, where he finds Kunikida fighting against a skill user.

◊ ◊ ◊

Facing the young man, I charge. Now that I've lost my pistol, close-quarters combat is my only chance to subdue him. The skill user steps backward, but I pursue and reach out to grab his arm. Most of the martial arts I know involves using the opponent's momentum against them, which is why I have to grab them first if they refuse to engage. I drag his arm to pull him off-balance before moving out of the way. Then I step in to grab him, but that's when I see him raise his arm into the air, and I come to a sudden stop.

—*Here comes another shock wave!*

Rolling to the side, I evade the ray coming from his arm. I dodge his attack, and yet, I don't. The wave knocks me back, and every bone in my body lets out a crack. My brain shakes, unable to keep up with the sudden acceleration of my body, and I start blacking out. I know I dodged his attack, so why—?

"Here's the thing about my attacks… You can't dodge them. I'm not hitting you with a shock wave. I'm able to accelerate those marked with the 'number' in any direction I want. Any direction I want. Any direction. Which is why—"

"Gwah?!"

My spine creaks. Following the swing of his arm, I am slammed into the ground. It feels as if gravity has suddenly been increased a hundredfold.

"Oh look, a fly!"

He lifts his arm into the air only to swing it down once more, crashing me into the floor like a flyswatter. He repeatedly slams me on the ground. It feels like being hit by a train over and over again. My bones crack; my skin tears. The numbers on my body have already decreased to "21."

"That number is how much time you have left to live! Once it reaches zero, you writhe in pain until you're dead! Nobody can escape their fate! Nobody! Nobody! Nobody! Nobody!"

The acceleration stops, but I'm unable to even lift a finger. It's as if every muscle in my body is torn. A warm liquid creeps into every breath.

"Give up yet, Detective?"

The young man casually approaches me as I remain lying on the ground, unable to move. It hurts to breathe. Every joint in my body is screaming in pain.

"I shoulda killed you all one by one like this from the start. I didn't need to go through the trouble of framing the mysterious newcomer to bring down the detective agency from the inside. Besides, that strategy failed anyway."

The young man stands next to me and casually kicks me in the head. I see stars, but I can't do anything about it.

"But it's always good to be optimistic. I'll kill you, *kill* you, and after that, I'll kill your friend upstairs—kill him, too. After that, the plane's gonna crash, and the detective agency's rep will be ruined, and that'll make my work in Yokohama a little easier. It'll make it a little easier, right?"

"Your work...?"

"I'm sick and tired of shuffling goods in secret while living in fear of private organizations of skill users like yours. I'm gonna live in a world where I can buy all the organs I need and sell all the weapons I want. I'll make a killing."

Organs...and weapons.

This is the organ-trafficking syndicate! If the Port Mafia are the sellers, then that would make these guys the buyers. They're an underground criminal organization and general trading company in the black market for illegal goods such as organs and weapons. They have countless smugglers under their banner and ties with criminal organizations domestically and internationally.

"I learned from the Azure King incident that the Armed Detective Agency isn't to be taken lightly. We're big on discretion. We crush our enemies before they're a threat. That's the basics of the basics of business."

The numbers on my body are now at "11." I guess whatever happened to the taxi driver and Alamta is going to happen to me if these reach "00."

"...You seem to be making good money selling weapons to foreign merchants."

"There's so much to like about this city: the Port Mafia, the conflict in the foreign communities, the lawless areas of Yokohama, and the fights just waiting to escalate. I love this place."

He's right. The fighting in this city will never disappear. An arms dealer such as him must feel like a ship's captain arriving at a new frontier. They buy organs or foolhardy thugs to sell to foreign syndicates, while bringing smuggled military weapons and seasoned mercenaries into the country to make a profit. And just like that, a new death trade is carried in from abroad to a world where the law and morals are meaningless.

However...

"I...cannot allow you to sell any more weapons. Even the smallest street fight could end with serious injuries or death if a dagger or firearm was brought into the equation. That's why—"

"Whoa, there. What d'you think you're doing?"

The enemy raises his arm, sending my body straight up. As the air is expelled from my lungs, the notebook I was hiding in my breast pocket slips out.

Shit!

"You thought you could buy some time talking so you could write in your notebook, huh? But that's not happening. That is not happening. I know what your skill is. Anyway, I'll be taking this."

He holds the notebook in the air and shakes it at me. My skill has two disadvantages: One is the fact that it takes time to write something in my notebook and rip out the page. The other...is the fact that I cannot use my skill at all if my notebook has been stolen.

Just like that, my skill has been completely neutralized. I still have my wire gun from the last fight tucked in my belt behind me, but it doesn't have enough power to kill, let alone seriously wound someone. Nevertheless, I cannot give up. That's the one thing I can't do. Not because I have to save the lives of the victims on the plane or because it's my job as a detective at the Armed Detective Agency, but because I've decided that's what needs to be done.

An agonizing pain shoots down my body, but I ignore it and get to my feet.

"Wow... Your eyes still got a little life in 'em, huh? Guess that means you want seconds!"

I take another hit from behind that spins me around and rams me into the ground.

"Gah...!"

I cough up blood. My vision blurs. I don't even know what kind of position my body is in anymore.

"And now for the grand finale. Here, I have a key. What key, you ask? The release key for the communicator. You won't be able to save the people on that airplane without this... You want it? You want it, don'cha?"

He pulls a thin key out of his pocket. It's a small and fragile key with a dull yellow tint. I gaze at it.

"Want it? Here ya go."

He bends the key *until it audibly snaps in half.*

"What—?"

"Ah-ha-ha-ha... Ha-ha-ha-ha! All hope is lost! Now nothing can prevent the plane from crashing! It's over! It's over, it's over, it's over! Ah-ha-ha-ha!"

The young man scornfully laughs—the wicked laugh of a man watching the world burn.

"Now, let's put an end to this. I'm gonna kill you. I'll kill you, and we will scream our victory from the mountaintops!"

He raises his hand. The number on me is now displaying "04."

I instinctively look up at the operations room on the second floor where I see Dazai. Dazai, bloodied and beaten...

⬡ ⬡ ⬡

Kunikida is outside the window, riddled with wounds. Dazai takes another blow to the face so powerful it shatters the window on impact. Fragments of glass scatter into the air.

Dazai looks at Kunikida, and their eyes meet. They yell.

⬡ ⬡ ⬡

"KUNIKIDA!"
"DAZAI!"

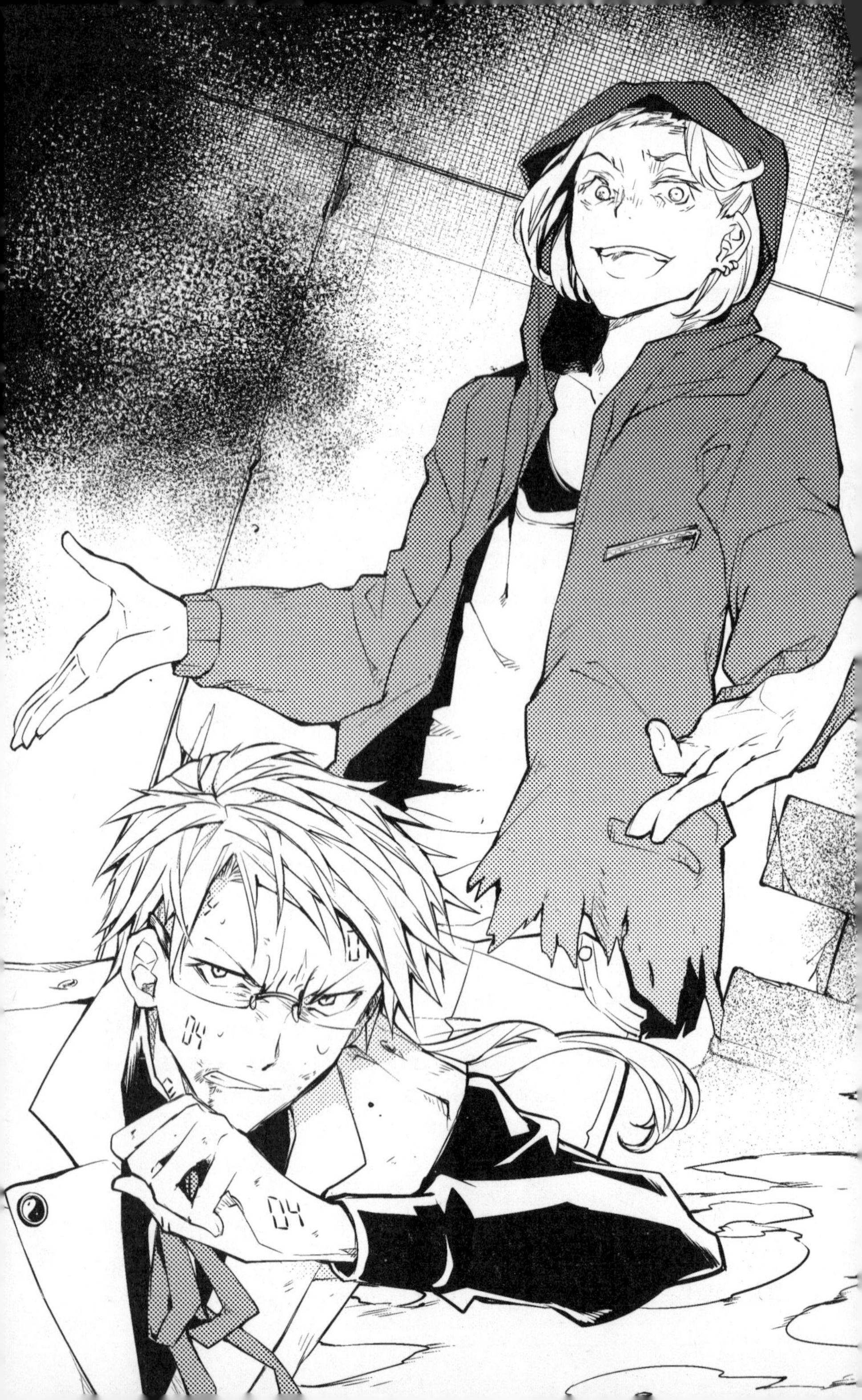

◇ ◇ ◇

That is all it takes. We know what to do.

I promptly pull out the wire gun at my waist and *shoot it at Dazai*. The hook hits the wall right next to him just as I wanted it to. Immediately, I reel in the wire, hoisting my body into the air.

◇ ◇ ◇

Dazai kicks off the window frame and leaps out the window. Kunikida's eyes are locked on him as he flies through the air at the end of the steel wire.

They exchange glances, then words, before the distance between them widens again.

◇ ◇ ◇

Utilizing the tensile force of the wire, I swiftly glide through the air. Dazai has already left the operations room and is falling toward the ground. After arriving at a point right under the window to the operations room, I continue letting the wire pull me up…

…*allowing me to run straight up the wall.*

"HAAAAAAH!"

Kicking off the wall, I lunge into the room. I look up and see a tanned giant of a man equipped with some sort of brass knuckles. A fist powerful enough to crush a person immediately swings past my head.

The behemoth is thrown into the air.

His path through the air carries him right into the wall. His face is overcome with astonishment and bewilderment. He has no idea I just used his momentum to throw him over my shoulder. However, the man soon stands back up and throws a second punch.

"You should have stayed down."

I roll with his attack and grab his wrist. Then, pulling him forward and off-balance, I gently cup his elbow while shifting my weight backward to lift him off the ground before throwing him along the wall and into the ceiling. His eyes roll back.

⬡ ⬡ ⬡

"What—?! You're…"

"Sorry, but you're up against me now."

After landing on the first floor, Dazai casually walks over to the young man.

"Why…?! Why won't any numbers appear?! I can't *accelerate*, either! Why, why, why is this happening?!"

"You should've done your homework. Skills don't work on me."

The enemy steps back while raising his hand, but Dazai, unconcerned, only continues to get closer.

"Explain yourself! How did you two know to switch opponents just by looking at each other?! What kinda trick was that?"

Wearing an unwavering smile, Dazai continues to close the distance. The young man steps back, overwhelmed.

"J-just who the hell are you?! Your entire history was wiped clean! Who are you?! Who?! Who?!"

"Oh, looks like I forgot to introduce myself."

Dazai towers over the young man and peers down at him. Then he gently clenches his fist before raising it into the air.

Dazai's right fist connects with the young man's face, spinning him a full 180 degrees. The enemy's eyes roll back into his head as he passes out.

* * *

"The name's Osamu Dazai, Armed Detective Agency personnel."

O O O

The giant man charges at me like a wild beast before I throw him into the air. The stronger my opponent, the more powerful the throw. After a few tosses, I eventually hurl him through the window frame, where he free-falls all the way down to the first floor.

When I glance out the window, I see that he's foaming at the mouth, out cold. He won't be waking up from that for a while. Then I look at my body to find that the numbers have vanished. Dazai must have defeated that skill user.

Phew. Thank goodness.

Relieved, I check the communicator. All that's left is to cut this machine off. I operate the vintage device, fumbling with the frequency and direction. It's a rather old machine, but I can manage.

"Kunikida!"

Dazai comes rushing up the stairs now that the enemy below is defeated.

"I think we need this release key to use the communicator! But it looks like that jerk broke it before passing out!"

Flustered, he shows me the bent key.

"I know."

"We can't work the communicator with this! The plane's—"

"I'm constantly running into issues. The unexpected is my norm. That's why…"

I tear the stitches off my hip pocket and pull out a sheet of paper.

"…I always have a spare page with me for emergencies."

I unfold the paper and write with my own blood.

"The Matchless Poet: Release Key!"

The piece of paper transforms into a yellow release key.

"And as long as I get one good look, I can produce a perfect replica using my skill."

"Wh-whoa… Really?" The unflappable Dazai finally opens his eyes wide in astonishment.

"Really. Surprised? I think you are. All right, we made a promise. You owe me a drink."

Operating the communicator's control panel, I adjust the settings, insert the release key, and turn it. Immediately afterward, a green light illuminates the control panel. I forcefully press the disable button.

"Now the airplane should have full control again! Dazai, call the pilot!"

"Already on it!"

We rush toward the outside, but at the same time, I can hear a low rumbling coming from somewhere. It's getting closer.

This sound—

It gradually grows louder until it becomes a deafening roar.

"Captain! Can you hear me?! We stopped the interference device! You should be able to control the plane now. Hurry! Pull up the nose and gain some altitude!"

"I'm trying! But we've already lost too much altitude! Damn it! Come on!"

The roaring that we're hearing is the passenger aircraft flying right above us!

Dazai and I race out of the building. A colossal shadow sweeps the ground as the heavens thunder overhead. I gaze into the sky.

It's getting closer! The airplane flies over us, gradually being sucked in by the land up ahead.

Heading toward the city… And down toward the earth…

Don't fall. You absolutely must not fall.

Don't fall. Fly to the sky! Fly!

"FLYYYYYYYYYYYYYYYY!!" I bellow.

* * *

The passenger aircraft's shadow grazes the ground before the nose pulls up. A surging gust storms across the land as the aircraft regains altitude, and the plane flies toward the evening sun.

—*It's flying.*

They made it.

Together, Dazai and I watch the airplane slowly melt into the deep-crimson sky.

CHAPTER IV

13th

I am writing this after returning home for the first time in a long while.

The simplest path in life is being satisfied with each day for what it is.

With the help of others, we saved those who were to die. Yet those who were not saved cannot be revived.

The truth. Problems stem from the truth. Deviating from the truth causes problems in the realm of men. The truth does not move people because living and dying are constants, regardless of any such truths.

Nobody knows these truths, for we cannot see them.

And with that, the case came to a close.

Since then, the agency and myself have been busy dealing with the aftermath of the events. Interviews with the police, insurance claims, dealing with news agencies: There are many clerical tasks that need my care, despite my job title as a private investigator. I'm so swamped with work that I lack even a moment to spare for sentimentality.

Perhaps realizing there was going to be a lot of office work needing to be done, Dazai said he had "something to look into" and immediately vanished into the ether. I'm going to throttle that man when I find him.

Many people witnessed the airplane almost crash. The news reported that it was the work of a foreign underground syndicate, and they added that our detective agency had a hand in the leader's arrest. While the Armed Detective Agency was praised for preventing an unprecedented disaster, there were also many who blamed us for the series of atrocious events because of our involvement. We will continue to receive backlash for the abandoned hospital incident in particular for some time.

One day, as I finish seeing to my usual piles of routine tasks and reports, the president summons me to his office.

"You called?" I bow before stepping in.

"How is work coming along?" the president asks, his eyes still fixed on the documents on his desk.

"Busy as always. And to make matters worse, Dazai ran off. He said he hates office work, then dumped all his paperwork onto one of our clerks. He's also somehow managed to avoid all the military investigation department's interviews. I think putting him in a pot of scalding water should set him straight. Not long enough to kill him, though. He'd like that."

"Just make sure to do it somewhere remote where the police won't find you."

The president gathers the documents and seals them in an envelope before looking at me.

"You did well. We even received a direct honorable mention from one of the MP's generals. He said, 'Your detective agency is what others should strive for.' This has taken some of the weight off my shoulders as well. For a moment...I was even considering closing down the agency permanently."

That's...

The president continues before I can say anything.

"There is no agency more valuable than human life. I thought if the continued existence of our organization put people's lives at risk, then ceasing operations would be for the best... However, everything has been solved. It's all thanks to your hard work, Kunikida."

He rubs his brow with his fingers. The president never expresses any work-related anxieties...but he must be slightly exhausted.

"So, Kunikida, did you find the answer to your homework?"

My homework.

—*The "entrance exam."*

...The task the president assigned me in order to deem whether Dazai is suitable for the agency.

"If you're asking about Dazai, then I already have my answer: That man is the worst. He ignores my orders, randomly disappears during work, is obsessed with suicide, flirts with every woman he sees, refuses to do physical labor, and is downright lazy. He is clearly unfit for society. He wouldn't make it three days at another job before being kicked out."

I briefly pause before delivering the verdict I prepared.

"...However, as a detective, he has exceptional talent. He will undoubtedly become the top detective at our agency within the next few years... He passed the test."

"I see. I trust your judgment."

The president's pen glides over the acceptance forms before he stamps them with his seal of approval. Osamu Dazai has officially been accepted into the detective agency.

"By the way, sir, if it wouldn't be a problem, I would like to request the rest of the day off."

"Do as you please. Is it something important?"

"I have...some business to attend to."

○ ◇ ◇

After passing through the grove, I arrive at a small cemetery overlooking the port. The small graves sparsely line up across the slope, bathed in the light reflected from the sea. I walk among the graves until I reach one that's new. I offer flowers, then put my hands together.

"Visiting a victim's grave, Detective Kunikida?" asks a clear voice.

I open my eyes at the sound and find Miss Sasaki dressed in a white kimono by my side. She holds a bouquet of white chrysanthemums in her right hand. After placing her flowers beside mine, she gently closes her eyes.

"You look even lovelier in a kimono."

"It probably would have been more appropriate to wear a mourning dress, but unfortunately, this is all I own... Detective Kunikida, do you always offer flowers to the graves of the victims?"

Miss Sasaki and I are here to honor those who were kidnapped and murdered in the basement of the abandoned hospital.

"Yes. There is no particular reason why I do it. I simply feel I should."

Without saying a word, she gazes at me and smiles. The trees on the forest path sway in the gentle ocean breeze. I continue, as if I were talking only to myself.

"...The first time someone died on the job, I cried so much that I couldn't get out of bed. I couldn't even call the agency to tell them I wasn't coming in. I thought I would never recover. And yet, now I don't even shed a single tear. That's why I come here instead. I feel like I need to do something so that the victims can rest in peace."

"Would shedding a single tear...help those who passed to rest in peace?"

"I don't know. Perhaps it doesn't do anything. Our calls will not reach the deceased, no matter how much we pray or sob before their graves. Time has stopped for them. All we can do is mourn and believe that we live in a world where it is normal for people to die and for the living to mourn them."

"...You're a cruel person, Detective Kunikida."

As I turn to face her, I'm taken by surprise. Tears well in her eyes as she tries not to cry.

"I lied to you the other day. The man I said I broke up with... He actually passed away. He was a man of ideals. I did everything I could to support him, yet...he died without ever telling me he loved me."

I'm sure a considerate person would be able to offer kind words of comfort during times like this.

"Oh." But all I offer her is one foolish, simple word.

"The departed are cowards. It is exactly as you say, Detective Kunikida. Time has stopped for the dead, and there is nothing we can do to bring them joy or make them smile. I'm— I've grown tired."

Unable to hold it in any longer, she lets a large teardrop slide down her cheek. If an all-knowing wise man knew the exact right words to say, would even he be able to stop those tears?

I don't know. I've gone through trials and tribulations to pursue my ideals, write them in my notebook, and make them a reality. Even now, I wonder if there exists a perfect word or a perfect salvation to save every single person on this planet. But such an endeavor means nothing before a lone woman's tears.

"I apologize. I let my emotions get the best of me... I should be going soon."

"Are you okay?"

A stupid question, I admit.

"Yes, I'm fine. I was actually asked to be a consulting analyst for this case by the military police. It is within my field of expertise, and this is a very complicated case...so I am meeting with the government official in charge after this."

Anyone who consults for the MP must be someone of top caliber. Even ignoring the fact that she had a hand in solving this case, she still must have an impressive track record in the field.

"Well, if I ever run into trouble at work, I will make sure to get in touch with you."

"Yes, please do."

She finally smiles. The breeze from over the horizon brushes past the mountain ridges. With a silent bow, she leaves. After watching her fade into the distance, I turn to the city of Yokohama and idly gaze at the scenery.

Suddenly, my phone rings, catching my attention. It's Dazai.

"Kunikida, I need you to come here."

His voice is unusually dark for a change.

◇   ◇   ◇

"What did you ask me to come here for?"

Dazai told me to meet him at the abandoned hospital where the first incident took place. Under the warmth of the sun, what the darkness had turned into an eerie, ominous abandoned hospital proves to be nothing more than a faded, deserted building. Radiant sunlight peeks through the shattered window of what used to be a sickroom, illuminating the floor.

"How in the world do you remove the safety on this gun?"

I look over. He has a gun, surprisingly enough. It's a compact pistol belonging to our agency that uses double-column magazines. Any employee of ours is free to borrow one.

"You called me all the way over here to ask me that?"

In awe of his stupidity, I remove the black pistol's safety. He aims the muzzle a few times at some empty space before opening his mouth again.

"Y'know, I have a hard time believing that arms dealer was the Azure Apostle."

—What?

"I mean, it has to be, right? There's no way they could've done all that on their own. Plus, what's the motive?"

"What about the reason they gave me? The Armed Detective Agency was getting in the way of their business in Yokohama, so they planned all this to get rid of us."

"Yeah, and that's probably what they believe, too. But is that really something they just had to do?"

"...What are you getting at?"

"Well, they saw the detective agency as a threat after the whole Azure King incident, but we're not the only armed organization that would get in their way. They'd have to keep an eye out for the military, the coast guard—and if we're talking skill users, the Home Affairs Ministry's Special Division for Unusual Powers. Don't you think it's a little overkill to cause such a scene just to go after the detective agency? It's not cost-effective."

"Get to the point."

"Somebody manipulated them—convinced them that the detective agency was their biggest threat."

Don't tell me that the real Azure Apostle is still out there, then?

"So tell me, Dazai. Do you already have an idea of who this person is?"

"Yep."

"Who is it?!"

I can't help grabbing Dazai by the collar, but he doesn't even bat an eye as he stares directly into mine.

"I e-mailed them and asked them to come here. Said I had evidence that they were the real culprit. They should be here any minute now."

What?

I survey the room.

It's extremely ordinary, most likely a sickroom at one point. The entrance is in front with a window in the back. Two rusted bed frames lie before us while an empty medicine cabinet stands by our side. There is nothing else in here. It's basically empty—not even much dirt or dust on the floor, either... The real culprit is coming *here* of all places?

"I hear footsteps," Dazai suddenly says.

I reflexively look to the entrance. I can hear them, too, one after another, slowly coming this way. I notice Dazai tightly holding the pistol. So that's why he brought it. I already returned my gun to the president. Should I use my notebook to make another? No, there's not enough time.

Sweat unexpectedly drips down my cheek. The footsteps are getting louder. They'll be here any second now. I see their feet—their body—their face—

"The hell are you doing here, Four-Eyes?"

The person standing at the entrance is...

"Why...are you here?"

"I oughta be asking you the same thing. Did you come here to find out the truth, too?"

Standing in the doorway is the young hacker Rokuzo.

—*Are you the one behind this?*

Are you the Azure Apostle?

My brain automatically jumps into gear. Rokuzo would indeed be able to remotely access Dazai's computer and send an e-mail. Not only that, my suspicions about Dazai stemmed from the information Rokuzo gave me. Furthermore, contacting foreign underground syndicates and providing biased information wouldn't be that difficult for an illegal hacker, either. And above all...he has a motive. He has a motive to resent the detective agency—a motive to resent me.

"Why, Rokuzo? Is it my fault? Is that it? Because it's my fault your father died—you resented me that much?"

"My father? Yeah, I hate the man who killed my dad. Obviously. But, Four-Eyes—"

Dazai suddenly speaks up. "It looks like some hacker was *reading my e-mails*, huh?"

What?
Dazai...I thought you said you e-mailed the real culprit?
Just then...

A gunshot.

A large hole opens in Rokuzo's chest.
Fresh blood sprays from the wound.

"_____"

Rokuzo collapses forward with his mouth open as if he was trying to tell me something.
He's been shot.
I automatically look at Dazai, but his gun is at his side. His expression is cold as well. I hear a voice coming from behind Rokuzo's body at the entrance.

"Detective Kunikida... I apologize."

A shadow appears before the doorway.
Long black hair. Delicate lips. A white kimono. A faintly smoking pistol in hand.
She walks over Rokuzo's body as she approaches us.
It's strange.
She was so...beautiful.
"So you're the Azure Apostle." My voice echoes in the room as if it belongs to someone else.
"Yes."
Her dignified tone, clear as a bell, causes my heart to skip a beat.
"So, Miss Sasaki...you admit you're the mastermind behind all this?" Dazai asks.
"Detective Dazai, I beg of you. Please...drop the gun. If you don't..."
She points the muzzle at him.

"How 'bout this: I'll get rid of the gun if you answer a few questions for me. Deal?"

"Certainly. Ask whatever you like."

"All right, I'm dropping the gun now." Dazai casually lets the gun fall to the floor with a clatter.

"Miss Sasaki, why did you target the detective agency?"

"I believe you know why, Detective Dazai."

"I'm impressed. You tried hiding it when we were around, but you're sharp. I can see why you're such a celebrated criminal psychology researcher at your age." He continues resignedly, "There are two things you wanted to do: one, punish criminals, and two, get your revenge on the detective agency. Am I right?"

Punish criminals? That sounds just like—

"This is...the only way I could think of."

"Was there even a point in taking revenge?"

"Detective Dazai, all revenge is meaningless. I just... I had to do it. Even though I knew it was wrong, I had to do it for *him* or else I felt I might lose control of myself."

Revenge?

A lot of people hold grudges against the detective agency. The number of those who want to take revenge on us is endless.

"You're right. Revenge is something you do despite knowing that it's meaningless. And unfortunately...you didn't have anyone else to exact revenge upon."

—*"He actually passed away."*

—*"He was a man of ideals."*

"Alone, you're helpless, but with your brain and knowledge of criminals, you were able to punish crooks for their wrongdoings time and time again. That's why this Azure Apostle plan was something you had to do."

Dazai pauses, then glances at me before speaking again.

"Every single action of yours was part of a vengeful crusade for your deceased lover—the Azure King."

*　　*　　*

The Azure King.

An unusual terrorist who committed crimes to punish criminals. The detective agency learned of his whereabouts...and now he's dead.

"There were whispers in the past speculating that he might've had an accomplice, given how intricate his crimes were. However, the authorities at the time concluded that while he may have hired some people to help carry out the crimes, there were no signs of an actual accomplice who shared his views. They based their conclusion on the fact that criminals generally band together for two reasons: because they share political views or because they're splitting the spoils of their crimes. But the Azure Banner Terrorist case wasn't about money or politics... Nobody even imagined that the Azure King had a romantic partner who was a far better strategist than he was."

"He was...a man of noble character. The rampant crime pained his heart. He tormented himself searching for a way to create an ideal world where nobody had to suffer. Once he realized that simply obeying the law couldn't save everyone, he aspired to join those who create the laws—a government official."

Miss Sasaki continues in a detached manner as if she is releasing pent-up emotions. "And yet, even then, it was a difficult path. The corrupt system, the interference of his colleagues, the misunderstandings from his boss—he was crushed. He agonized over it, and every time he got up, he was knocked back down. Just watching him, I could see that this path he had chosen was no different from walking barefoot over a bed of nails. Then, one day, he simply had enough. He lost his way, unable to realize his ideals, so he tried to slice open his stomach and kill himself. Unable to bear it...I devised an unspeakable plan."

Dirtying one's own hands to punish the wicked...

Walking a path of carnage to realize one's ideals...

"Miss Sasaki, would I be correct to assume that most of the

crimes the Azure King committed were your idea? You did it for the man you loved."

"And I don't regret it," she states clearly. "His ideals are my ideals. I would commit acts of pure evil with bloodstained hands just to bring them to fruition."

"But the Azure King is dead. The detective agency had him cornered, and he killed himself along with Rokuzo's father. It should've ended then."

"No, it couldn't be stopped. The plan was only halfway finished back then. There were criminals who still needed to be punished. And...perhaps you will laugh at me, but when faced with the reality of his death, I simply couldn't live with my own inaction any longer."

"So you came up with a plan to get the remaining criminals to *voluntarily commit crimes* so that our detective agency would punish them. You predicted that we'd have to pursue and arrest them if you created a scandal."

The taxi driver left no evidence of his kidnappings, the bomber Alamta didn't even exist in Japan as far as the records showed, and the arms dealer was involved in organ trafficking, secretly trying to import weapons. Each case involving these invisible criminals would be extremely difficult to take to court with the current laws and regulations in place.

"The most beautiful thing about your scheme is that you never had to dirty your own hands. In fact, I bet you even had the arms dealers set up the surveillance equipment, prepare an area to confine the kidnapped victims, and make a deal with the bomber Alamta. I bet you didn't even lift a finger. Even until the very end, the arms dealer and his group believed they were doing everything of their own free will. That's why there was no evidence. Not even the arms dealers figured out how you, the initial source of the information, intentionally misrepresented the situation. That's why the only conclusion the authorities could come to was that this was a mishandling of information among arms dealers."

I felt it when I was pursuing the kidnapper and when I was questioning Dazai: The person behind this will not soil their own hands. A criminal who has committed no crimes cannot be judged by the law.

—*Is that really okay?*

—*Is a world that allows such injustice forgivable?*

"Then you pretended to be one of the kidnapped victims so that we wouldn't even doubt you. It was also how you initiated contact with the detective agency. *You were the only one the taxi driver didn't kidnap.* Everything seemed to make sense, so we didn't press you for answers at the time, but there was absolutely no reason for the kidnapper to go out of his way to abduct a woman who fainted at the train station, especially when there were many witnesses. He already had a low-risk plan that worked, which was to kidnap people on their way to their hotel. Also, if he claimed he didn't know you, then he'd basically be confessing that he knew the other victims, and that's why he couldn't say anything. And just like that, you played on everyone's emotions until you brilliantly sneaked into the detective agency."

There is a deep crevice now between Dazai's eyebrows.

"Miss Sasaki, I just don't understand. Someone as smart as you could have accomplished so much in criminal psychology. Or you could've even gotten involved in the government's criminal investigation system and created a more advanced crime-fighting organization. I'm not saying it would've been perfect, but the world would've at least been a better place because of it. And yet..."

"I...have no ambitions of my own. I just didn't want to see him in pain anymore."

Why?

One question continues to spin in the back of my head.

Just why?

Who is wrong? Who betrayed their ideals?

"Miss Sasaki, it's over. Despite working so hard not to dirty your hands—to be invisible—you won't be able to cover up kill-ing Rokuzo. We're witnesses, and you'll be tried under the full extent of the existing laws."

"I am afraid not."

She points the muzzle at Dazai.

Absurd... Does she really think she can threaten us with that after all that's happened?

"There will not be any witnesses, and you will not be able to testify. Because if you tell anyone what happened here, *I will resume my attack against the detective agency.*"

A slight smile rises to Miss Sasaki's eyes as she threatens us. *Did she calculate even this outcome beforehand—?*

"Stop."

The hoarse word rises out of my dry throat.

"Stop. It's over. I will not allow you to attack the detective agency ever again."

"Please, Detective Kunikida, don't move."

"Stop! Why?! Why are you doing this?! We're not the ones you should be aiming your gun at!"

"Then tell me. Who should I be pointing it at? Who should I despise?"

"That's—"

Is there anyone who fits the bill? The cause of all this? There has to be an ideal world where everyone can be saved, and there has to be something sinister blocking that path. There must be something... I'm sure of it...

Perhaps taking my hesitation as the absence of an answer, she frowns and looks away.

"As in the past, I will continue to be the one who fights for his ideals—the Azure King's ideals. And you, the detective agency, will not be able to stop that. That's why..."

Miss Sasaki slowly lowers the gun.

"Let's make a deal. You promise to leave me alone, and I prom-ise I won't attack the agency. I will go somewhere else, use another organization, and do the same thing. And after that, I will do it again...and again after that. I will not allow you to get in my way."

"That's it?"

Dazai turns a piercing gaze on Miss Sasaki.

"You of all people should understand, Detective Dazai. You always think ahead, doing whatever produces optimal results without being swayed by your emotions. Meaning you should know there is only one option here."

"You're absolutely right. I'm not going to do anything."

"...Farewell."

Miss Sasaki gazes into my eyes, then faintly smiles. Will she really continue doing this—deceiving others, manipulating criminals, and leaving countless bodies behind as the Azure Apostle, following in the steps of a ghost?

—*"Time has stopped for the dead, and there is nothing we can do to bring them joy or make them smile."*

—*"I've grown tired."*

I cannot allow her to kill anyone. That is not what's ideal, and an ideal world unquestionably exists. Who is at fault here? What do I have to do to find the answer? How can I reach these ideals?

"Detective Kunikida," she whispers. "When you saved me in the basement...you didn't even hesitate for a moment to pull me out from that water tank. While I may have been deceiving you...what you did...made me happy. Since this is the last time we will ever meet, I have one last thing I want to tell you, Detective Kunikida."

Gunshots.

Three bullets pierce Miss Sasaki's chest.

Blood sprays from the holes in her bosom.

She twirls in her white kimono like a flower petal fluttering in the wind.

Then, just like a marionette cut from its strings—

"Sasaki!"

I rush over and lift up her body. She's light, reminiscent of a porcelain doll. The blood flows from her wounds, staining her kimono crimson.

"Eat...shit..."

I look up. A black pistol rests in Rokuzo's hand as he lies collapsed on the floor.

"You...and the Azure King... You killed...my father...!"

Gun smoke rises into the air. A fierce smirk crosses Rokuzo's pale lips as he lies in a pool of his own blood.

"That was...for my father...! He stood...for justice! Eat shit and...die...!"

The gun falls out of Rokuzo's hand, and his face drops into the red puddle. He faintly twitches...and goes still.

"Detec...tive...Kuni...kida..."

Miss Sasaki whispers in my arms. A drop of blood gently slides out of the corner of her mouth.

"Something about you...reminds me of him..."

Her dark-brown eyes tremble as they reflect the light.

"Please...don't let...your ideals...kill you...... I.........love......"

....

She's dead.

"Kunikida, she killed too many people. This is how it had to be."

Blood rushes to my head.

"DAZAI!"

I tightly seize him by the lapels, but he doesn't even blink. All he does is gaze back into my raging eyes.

"Kunikida, the ideal world you're after doesn't exist. Give it up."

"Shut up! She was just one woman! She hardly even knew how to use a gun! There was no reason to kill her! If you would have given us some time to plan, we could have found a way where nobody else had to die! Why...?!"

"I wasn't the one who killed her. That was Rokuzo."

"Did you think I wouldn't notice?!" I point to the black pistol lying beside Rokuzo. "*That's your gun!* You kicked it over to Rokuzo when I was talking to her because you knew he would kill her!"

From where Dazai is standing, he could kick the gun under the bed to Rokuzo without Miss Sasaki noticing.

"I didn't kill her."

"Indirectly, you did!"

"Sorry, but you can't prove that I had any intention to. The one who held the gun and pulled the trigger with the intent to kill was Rokuzo. All I did was trip on a gun that was lying on the ground."

A murderer who doesn't soil their own hands...

Getting someone to kill another human being for you: What Dazai did was no different from what Miss Sasaki did. There is no way to prove their intention to kill under current laws and regulations, and they would go unpunished.

"Kunikida, that was the only way to save her. This was the best we could have hoped for."

"You're wrong!" I scream. "There is no way this is ideal or even good! There must have been something we could have done. There must have been a real underlying problem we just weren't seeing! Because..."

If Miss Sasaki really resented the world...

...if she really wanted to eliminate us...

...then she wouldn't have stopped me when I tried to walk into the poison gas. If she hadn't, I would have breathed it in and died. If she wanted revenge, then she could have easily killed me then. She could have made it look like an accident, and nobody would have doubted her.

But she saved me. Why? Was it…on instinct? A reflex?

Struggling to speak, I hit Dazai with the facts. "Because *the truth is, she didn't want to do any of this*! She had no interest in a world where criminals were killed for their crimes! She just…"

—"*I just didn't want to see him in pain anymore.*"

—"*You mustn't touch the lock!*"

"Tell me! Was it right for her to be shot and killed?! Is this the ideal world I seek?!"

Dazai just looks at me as he softly strings his words together.

"Kunikida, people who believe there is a right and a wrong—people who believe in the existence of an ideal world—they're the ones who end up resenting the world and hurting those around them when things don't go the way they want…just like the Azure King. When those ideals and beliefs are carried out, the victims are the weak and defenseless."

He stares off into the distance.

"A cry for righteousness is like a sword. Just as it may harm the weak, it will also never be able to protect or save them. The Azure King's righteousness is what killed Miss Sasaki."

Dazai's criticism drives deep. I was chasing after righteousness and ideals. I was able to rise above all adversity in order to realize them.

"Kunikida. As long as you continue to pursue those ideals and remove those who get in your way, then one day you, too, will come to harbor the Azure King's rage. There will be nothing left around you then—only ash. I've seen it happen all too often."

It is as if he's staring at something only he can see—something beyond my comprehension, like the abysmal darkness that resides in every human's heart.

"I…"

I let go of Dazai. I understand what he's saying. Perhaps righteousness isn't something you seek in others but something you search for inside yourself.

Even then...

Miss Sasaki is dead, and so is Rokuzo.

All I've found in my search for righteousness within myself is a sense of hopelessness.

"......"

I gaze out the abandoned hospital's window. The crimson spider lilies sway in the decaying garden out front. Even if I close my eyes, the flowers are still there, burned on the back of my eyelids...along with a trace of her smile.

INTERLUDE II

Nightfall.

Tilted on its side, a police van burns on the street alongside the coast facing the Yokohama harbor. Two officers lie dead under the shaking car.

"W-wait! Wh-what does the M-Mafia want with me?!"

Two more figures are still alive. One is a young arms dealer. He was arrested and in the middle of being transported to a military police facility when he was attacked and injured.

"You really don't know? How absurd."

The only other living soul, approaching the young man, is a dark shadow cloaked in a wriggling overcoat—Akutagawa.

"You disrespected the Port Mafia. You purposely fed us information on that organ-trafficking cabdriver so that we would dispose of him for you. Every person who has ever deceived us for personal gain has paid the price, and this time will be no different."

The young man falls on his rear as Akutagawa's black boots get closer.

"N-nobody! Nobody can kill me! Die!"

Right as the young man lifts his arm into the air, a tattoo-like pattern appears on Akutagawa's skin. The number is "21." Then, as he swings his arm, he swiftly accelerates Akutagawa backward. However...

"What—?!"

Although Akutagawa was knocked back, he gently stops before slowly returning to where he had been standing, unfazed.

"Is that it?"

His overcoat transformed into countless black needles that pierced the ground, acting as a cushion to support his body and soften the impact.

The two-headed beast Rashomon arises from the overcoat and soars in the arms dealer's direction. The young man tries to dodge, but he is too late, and the cloaked hound's razor-sharp jaws tear him apart. He screams in agony until he is nothing more than a pile of meat. Akutagawa coldly continues to watch.

"Wow, there goes my appetite."

He turns around to see a shadowy figure behind him.

Akutagawa immediately releases Rashomon's dark blades. The blades, sharp enough to slice through metal, shoot toward the shadowy figure's neck but are deflected by some invisible force the moment they connect. Rashomon's fangs claimed only a few layers of skin before they were blocked by a skill.

"Hey, where are your manners? We're business partners, are we not?"

"That still doesn't change the fact that you used the Port Mafia for your own personal gain."

A middle-aged Caucasian man wearing a black cap walks out from the shadows—the same American agent Dazai and Kunikida met at the embassy. The agent scratches his neck as he addresses Akutagawa casually.

"This is some sort of misunderstanding. I'm a client of yours, in a sense. You get the foreign trade route that young arms dealer once had, and we get to say we prevented an illegal exporter from our country from stirring up trouble in Japan. It's a fair deal if you ask me. So could you quit acting like I stole from you?"

"Deceiving and instigating is common practice for agents. I am sure you have other reasons for getting involved."

"Well, yeah, we do. But don't you worry about a thing. It's over," the agent continues with a smile. "I can't even begin to tell you how spooked we were when the Azure King started killing people. See, one of the lawmakers he executed was *an illegal collaborator we'd had in our pocket*. That Azure King probably had no idea, but it would have come out if the case dragged on too long. That's why we needed him to retire permanently...which is why we decided to investigate the case behind the scenes and *tip off the Armed Detective Agency about his whereabouts*. Of course, we falsified the source of the information. Then we fed the police investigation headquarters faulty intel to create confusion within the chain of command. It went exactly how we planned. The Azure King was surrounded by a few police officers, so he blew himself up and died. The truth remains shrouded in mystery, and everyone was relieved knowing the dangerous criminal was gone. A happy ending for us all."

After taking a few moments to ruminate over what the agent said, Akutagawa opens his mouth.

"Setting aside the arms dealer, I have a hard time believing a foreign intelligence agency would kill a Japanese terrorist to protect a secret. Why did you do it?"

"Oh, it's got nothing to do with any governmental intelligence agency. I belong to another group as well. We call ourselves the Guild."

"A double agent? How cliché."

"It's a side business of mine. Every member in the Guild's got a day job." The agent turns on his heel, then begins to walk away. "I'll probably be getting in touch with the Mafia again soon with another job. Until then."

Akutagawa sternly watches the agent go. "Wait. I'd like to ask you something."

The agent stops in his tracks.

"I'm looking for someone. He has the ability to nullify others' skills upon contact. Know anybody like that?"

"Sorry, afraid not."

"Then get out of my sight."

"You got it."

He begins to walk again before disappearing into the darkness of the evening twilight.

"...Where did you go? Why did you suddenly disappear?" Akutagawa soliloquizes, alone on the street. "For a moment, I thought you might have been the Azure King, but I was wrong. Where are you? There's no way you're dead. You are somewhere here in Yokohama. I just know it."

The winds of the night collect his words and carry them away.

"I'll find my mentor if it's the last thing I do. I'll find you, *former Port Mafia executive Dazai.*"

EPILOGUE

I sit before my desk at the office and flip through my notebook.

"And that's how the Azure Apostle was stopped. It's been two years since then."

I close my notebook, concluding the long story.

"So that was your first case with Dazai, huh?" Tanizaki says in admiration.

"Yes, and he hasn't changed at all since. He is still the same arrogant nuisance as he was then. We have work to do today, and yet, he's nowhere to be found... Naomi, have you traced the signal on that transmitter yet?"

"I did. It hasn't moved for around twenty minutes. It's coming from...I guess that's the river."

The river?

Naomi peers at a map. The coin-shaped tracker I gave Dazai is silently resting in the middle of the river. I take a moment to ponder.

"I know what happened. That idiot must have randomly jumped into the river with the tracker in his wallet, which probably fell out of his pocket and sunk to the bottom while Dazai floated farther downstream."

He and I are in the middle of an investigation, and we had been talking over the phone when he suddenly said, "What a nice river," and the line cut out. I was wondering what that was all about...

How much trouble does that suicide maniac have to cause me until he's satisfied?

"I'm going to go look for the freak. Honestly, it's a damn shame I have to search for my partner before I can get any real work done."

"Be careful out there, Kunikida. What are you investigating today?" Junichiro asks after getting out of his chair.

"We're searching for a *tiger*. There's a 'man-eating tiger' on the loose in Yokohama."

It's a difficult job, but even then...

—*He will undoubtedly become the top detective at our agency within the next few years.*

Even then, it should be an easy case for Dazai to solve.

My notebook in hand, I leave the detective agency. The evening light slowly makes its advance from the horizon, splitting Yokohama's sky into blue and crimson. A familiar scent accompanies the wind, tickling my nose, and I stop in my tracks.

I gaze down the block.

There is the street, the people, and at times, crime and sorrow.

Every time I run into such sadness, my ideals are battered, my words lose meaning, and my very heart bleeds.

Chasing ideals is a fruitless, difficult path.

And yet, even then...

Surrendering myself to the bustling city of Yokohama, I continue on.

AFTERWORD

It is a pleasure to meet you, and if this isn't the first time we've met, then it is nice to see you again! Kafka Asagiri here. I write the stories for the manga *Bungo Stray Dogs*. They usually go a little something like this:

DAZAI: "Hey, Atsushi. Just finishing up work for the day?" Dazai smiles cheerfully.
ATSUSHI: "D-did you...try to drown yourself again?" Atsushi makes a face.

That's my typical sloppy writing, but illustrator Sango Harukawa is the one who really makes the characters come to life. Her artwork makes things easy for me. But this time, things were different.

I had to take responsibility for every sentence I wrote in this novel. Everything from describing a cup on a table to an old man in town, I had to edit, adjust, and call the shots myself. If I was to describe my work on the manga in film terms, I would say that illustrator Harukawa is the actor, cameraperson, sound mixer, lighting technician, and scene editor, while all I do is write the scenario and help with the directing. That's why this book was such a huge task and a massive responsibility. The pressure from writing my first novel was so intense that I was trembling almost the entire time, like a phone on vibrate mode. But it was worth it in the end. In a sense, I was able to create a world that was richer than the comics, which I hope you enjoyed.

This novel is a spin-off about events that took place two years prior to the *Bungo Stray Dogs* manga. However, I wrote it in a way that you wouldn't need any prior knowledge of the series to enjoy the suspense and surprise. Additionally, I plan on writing a second novel that details the Port Mafia's past. The pressure and responsibility is already making me tremble so much that my table's legs are probably about to snap. I plan on finishing it before I dig a hole in the floor, so please look forward to it.

Finally, I would just like to thank a few people: Katou, the chief editor of the manga; Koshikawa, the chief editor of this novel, from Beans Bunko; Sango Harukawa, who always draws such stylish covers and characters (and without her illustrations, this novel would've just looked like some weird *Bungo Stray Dogs* rip-off!); and the advertisers, agencies, bookstores, and you, the reader! Thank you all so much.

Let us meet again in the next volume.

KAFKA ASAGIRI